Every Captive Freed

B.D. Lawrence,
Shannon McNear,
and
Angela D. Shelton

Edited by Sarah Everest
Cover by Kelsey Gietl
ISBN: 979-8-9991324-1-3

Sarah's Story

by B.D. Lawrence

Chapter 1

Sara Hanley entered the opulent sitting room and sat on the white, brushed fabric sofa.

"There she is." Marsha smiled at Sara. "The birthday girl. Happy birthday, sister."

"Thanks. Only the third time I remember anyone saying that to me."

"You're kidding?"

"Nope." Today had been like all the other birthdays she remembered. No presents. No party. No big deal. But she felt contentment. Even bordered on happiness. Filled with the joy of God.

"What are you, eighteen, right?"

Sara nodded. She felt thirty.

"So young." Marsha was the only other woman currently living in Calvin Rockport's palatial estate in the Huntleigh Woods section of St. Louis. She had a round face, small nose, and puffy cheeks.

Sara loved Marsha's Dutch-boy haircut but could not see herself with that style. "Yeah, like you're some ancient crone." Sara laughed.

"Twenty-four, girl."

"Ooh. Compared to our host, still a child."

"Everyone's young compared to Rockport."

Both women laughed.

"And you're a woman now." Marsha straightened and shimmied her shoulders. "Not a little girl anymore."

Woman? Wow. Sara never thought she'd make it to be a woman. She'd always thought she'd die as a girl on the streets or in some dive strip joint. But here she was with her first best friend in a living room that dwarfed the apartments and duplexes she'd been raised in. The modern furniture, plush chairs, soft beds, full kitchen, and swimming pool were things of dreams she'd had as a youngster, shuffling from foster home to foster home.

"Speaking of the men, where'd they go?" Sara asked.

Marsha filed her impressive nails. "Some nightclub"

"What nightclub?" Sara shivered. Bad memories.

Marsha looked up. "A little harsh, girl. You okay?"

"Sorry. Bad stuff going through my brain."

Marsha flashed a sympathetic smile. "They didn't say. East side, I think."

To shake off the sudden fear and queasiness, Sara pushed off the sofa and headed to the kitchen for a snack. Before she made it, the front door opened.

Calvin Rockport walked in. The man of about sixty, with mostly gray hair and a goatee, held the door for Chester, who entered carrying a young girl. She wriggled and moaned in his massive arms. Tall, black as midnight, with gentle brown eyes, Chester had been with Rockport for a of couple years longer than Sara. She credited the large man for making it through the first month. He'd not only helped her, but he'd also prevented her from leaving. And she'd tried several times.

Rockport smiled at Sara. "We got you a present. Happy birthday."

Someone else remembered. Sara frowned, unsure how a semi-conscious girl could be a birthday present. Had they found her on the street like that or had they snatched her from somewhere? "Who is she?" Sara pointed at the girl.

Chester carried her into the living room and laid her gently on the white sofa. The girl continued moaning. She rolled back and forth. Chester stayed by her to make sure she didn't fall off.

Marsha stood and placed her nail file on the fireplace mantel. She bent over the girl. "What's she on?"

Sara joined them. "Where'd you get her?"

"Keyshawn Williams's strip joint in East St. Louis," Chester answered.

"What? Are you two crazy? You carried a girl out of Keyshawn's place, and he didn't stop you?"

Chester answered Marsha," Meth, we think."

"Yeah, if it was Keyshawn's it'd be meth," Sara agreed. "Cheaper than H." Another nightmare memory steamrolled through her brain. She'd consumed her share of heroin when working in Keyshawn's club.

Rockport came alongside Sara. He put a hand on her shoulder.

Sara startled then turned on him. "You? You went into that strip club? No way their bouncer would let you in without an upfront payout. Old white rich dudes don't go to Keyshawn's places."

" Chester went in. Bought the girl. Took her into the back rooms. You know they have these rooms—"

"Yeah, I'm way too familiar with the set up."

"That's right. You worked there, didn't you?"

Sara shuddered, then nodded. Relentless memories abused her tired brain.

"Chester picked her up and carried her out the back door. I was waiting with the car."

Sara shook her head. Crazy old fools. "You know, don't you, that Keyshawn doesn't own squat? Big Eddie owns the clubs. He owns the girls, and he owns Keyshawn. Not the dude we want mad at us."

"He owned you, too, didn't he?"

Sara nodded. Weirdly, her memories of Big Eddie waffled between horrific and tolerable.

"And has anyone come looking for you?" Rockport bent over the moaning girl.

Her eyes opened wide. She thrashed on the sofa. Marsha held her shoulders down. The girl kicked her legs and tried to buck Marsha off her. "Lemego, lemego, lemego." Spittle sprayed from her mouth.

Sara backed away, not wanting anything to do with restraining the girl. The memories of her first night at Rockport's played through her mind. A stark contrast to the scene unfolding.

Rockport said, "Take her downstairs, Chester, would you? And Marsha, do your thing."

Chester leaned over and scooped the girl off the sofa. She continued thrashing, but Chester held her tight. He fast walked toward the kitchen and the basement stairs. Marsha ran upstairs to get her medical bag. Sara trotted past Chester and opened the basement door. The girl's moans and cries echoed all the way down the stairs. A door slammed, and the moans tapered to muffled cries. Marsha slipped past Sara and hurried down the stairs, a hypodermic with sedative at the ready.

Rockport joined Sara at the basement entrance. "In a few days it will be your turn. Convince that girl to stay here. Help her leave the life."

"You kidnapped her."

"We kidnapped you. And look how that turned out. Sara, that girl can't be more than fifteen. Help her."

"You're so old, dude. That girl isn't any older than thirteen."

Chapter 2

A few days turned into two weeks. Finally, the screaming tapered to moaning. The banging on the walls ceased. The girl downstairs started eating regularly. Marsha declared her ready for a conversation. Sara inched down the stairs. Snakes crawled in her belly. What would she say to Ashley? And why would this thirteen-year-old listen to her anyway? Why didn't Rockport ask Marsha to do this?

She knocked on the door to the plywood room. Another girl Rockport and Chester had grabbed several months ago had trashed the upstairs bedroom, so Chester had built a room in the basement to hold the girls during their first couple of weeks.

After a soft, "Come in," Sara eased open the door and walked into the room, closing the door behind her, locking her in with Ashley. Marsha had said she'd check on Sara in an hour.

The young girl sat up on the twin mattress. Long black hair. Tinted skin of some mixed ethnic origin. A pretty face. Full lips, sunken cheeks, and a wide nose. Her haunting eyes froze Sara. Despair, sadness, and abandonment oozed out of them. Had that been how she herself had looked nine months ago after spending several days locked in an upstairs bedroom? Probably.

The similarity ended there. Ashley cowered into the corner of the bed, knees under her chin, arms wrapped around her legs, eyes darting around the room. Every time someone had opened the door on Sara those first few weeks, she'd spewed streams of obscenities. And on a couple of occasions, she'd launched herself at Rockport only to smash into the brick wall named Chester Henderson.

"It's okay, Ashley. I'm not going to hurt you. Or stick you with anything." Sara held her empty hands up and showed them to the frightened girl. "Can I sit on the bed?"

A tentative nod.

Sara sat. She waited. Neither one spoke. Sara told herself she wanted Ashley to be comfortable and not afraid. The lie almost worked.

She wondered who was more afraid. What if she said something that messed up this young girl? She had to say something. But what would she tell this girl that could help?

Sara sighed. "We want to help you, Ashley. Get out of the life. Start over."

Ashley shook her head. "You don't know nothing about me. You don't know what my life is like. You don't know what they'll do to me when I go back."

Sara let out a small laugh.

"It's not funny." Tears leaked from the corners of Ashley's eyes.

Sara scooted closer and put her hand on the girl's knee. "I'm not laughing at you, hon. I'm laughing at what you said."

"Why?"

Here it was. She'd only shared her life story with Marsha, after she had agreed to stay at Rockport's and help. Sara bowed her head and silently prayed, "Lord please give me the words to touch Ashley's heart and help me not to say something that would hurt her."

Sara lifted her head and hoped she projected a concerned look. "Hon, I know exactly what you've gone through. And I know the people who think they own you. And I know what your life was like."

Ashley straightened and slid her legs down. Her incredible eyes widened. "How do you know this?"

"When I was twelve years old…"

*****

6 years ago

Sara Hanley leaned against the brick separating the two garden level apartment windows. The one to her left opened into the Garcia's bedroom. She knew because Sr. Garcia had taken her there a couple times. To her right was the Garcia's living room. The warm April breeze ruffled Sara's long blonde hair. Through the open living room window,

Sara heard every word spewing from the couple. They screamed at each other in Spanish, but Sara understood them, having spent the last nine years in various foster homes in the Pilsen neighborhood in the Lower West side of Chicago. Most of her foster families had been Mexican American. She'd been told her father was as well. But she didn't know. She went on what her mother had told her, combined with a vague memory of a bearded, dark-haired man coming and going during her early years.

"How could you sleep with her?" Sra. Garcia yelled at Sr. Garcia.

Jorge Garcia answered, "She came on to me. I . . . I had a moment of weakness. I'm so sorry."

"She's only twelve!"

"What? She told me she was eighteen."

"Does she look eighteen?"

"Yes, she looks like she could be eighteen."

Sara smiled, enjoying that last comment. Her breasts had come out early, about a year ago. She'd started her period, and her makeup made her look older. It hadn't been hard to convince Jorge Garcia she was eighteen when he came onto her. His pretending not to know made her laugh. She'd told him how old she was after they'd done it. Then she'd immediately told him she wanted one hundred dollars. That was three weeks ago. She'd collected one-hundred dollars from him twice a week for the past three weeks. But the cash stopped when Imelda Garcia discovered they were missing a lot of money.

"Why did you pay her six-hundred dollars? Is she a prostitute?"

Sr. Garcia did not respond.

"Then why did you pay her?"

Sr. Garcia swore. A door slammed. Sra. Garcia cried. Sara pushed off the wall, disappointed that her gig had ended. The six hundred dollars stuffed into her gym bag back at the house would help get her by, making up for receiving basically nothing but meals from her foster family. The disappointment faded into relief. She hated that dirty old man.

She strolled along the sidewalk of 19ᵗʰ Street toward her foster parents 'house. Early afternoon on a weekday, few other people were around. She'd skipped last hour at school. Study hall. No point going to that. Like she'd study. Boring.

Some robins dug for worms in the grass parkway. Vehicles zipped by. The smell of rotting eggs filled the air from the exhaust. A car horn blared, followed by a catcall. The usual thing that happened when she walked the streets. She ignored the lewd comments yelled at her from the passing car. If they stopped and bothered her, she could take care of herself. Her boyfriend Jesse had taught her some moves. And with her height and solid body, she had a chance against anyone who might bother her. And if not, they'd face the wrath of Jesse. He'd hunt them down and pulverize them.

As she passed the ancient Zion Evangelical Lutheran church, known as the ghost church, she shuddered, a sudden chill coming on her. Not a ghost. She didn't believe in them. Her history teacher had told her about the abandoned building. Built in the 1880s. Only the front wall and the bell tower remained. An iron fence enclosed a park known as "The Sanctuary". She'd never been through the locked doors, nor had she climbed the fence into the garden like other kids she knew. Usually on a dare. She didn't do dares. Nothing to prove.

As she hurried past, she glanced at the stairs leading up to the closed doors. A man on the top step watched her. He wore a white outfit with a red scarf hanging down both sides. Some kind of priest? He held his arms out toward her. She looked away but stopped after several steps and glanced back. No one stood on the steps. She shivered. Not a ghost. Just some dude.

She jogged the last block and a half to her current foster home. At least for now. How long would this family keep her around?

When she walked into the foyer of the two-story light brown brick house, her foster mother came out of the kitchen. A disappointed expression decorated her face. Nothing new there. Then her foster father came out. He frowned. His brows scrunched and his eyes narrowed.

Camila Martinez shook her head and approached Sara. She wore an apron over her ankle-length flower-patterned dress.

"Sara, why? Sra. Garcia called us. Why did you let Jorge Garcia take you? Why didn't you tell us he did this?"

"He didn't do anything. I did it." Sara held eye contact with Sra. Martinez, forcing the stout mid-thirties lady to look away.

Sr. Martinez came closer. "What do you mean? Are you saying you seduced Jorge?"

Sra. Martinez crossed herself and mumbled a prayer.

"Yup." Sara brushed past them and started up the stairs.

Sra. Martinez asked, "How could you give up your virginity to that man?"

Sara stopped and turned. "Virginity? I wasn't a virgin. Tomas Gomez took that two years ago." A well of anger rose in her. That fourteen-year-old brute. He'd told her he loved her, but she'd seen him with Amelia, his arm draped over her shoulder, walking down the alley, whispering in her ear. She'd gotten him back, though. He'd limp the rest of his life.

The Martinezes waved as Sara walked to the social worker's car parked on the street. Sara ignored them and tried to remember the social worker's name. Not that she cared. It came to her. Maria.

"It's not a long drive," Maria said. "Can I help you with your bag?"

Sara turned to the side, shielding the bag with her body. "I got it." She climbed into the back of the four-door car.

The Martinezes had treated her kindly. She had to admit that much. But obviously they hated her for what she'd done with Jorge Garcia. But at least she had the money she'd coerced out of that sick old man.

Maria drove them about a mile west and then a couple blocks south. Sara grew angry, knowing they'd kept her in the same neighborhood. Why? Just because she'd grown up in that area didn't mean she wanted to stay there.

"Why here?" she asked.

Maria parked on the street outside a brown brick apartment building that looked just like all the others she'd lived in. Two stories and a garden level. Two side-by-side entrances.

"These people have had three young girls foster with them. They're good people."

"Mexican?"

"No. They're Caucasian."

"White?"

"Yes, that means white."

They walked up the eight concrete steps to the left door. Maria opened the door and allowed Sara to enter first. The social worker pushed a little black button by a mailbox labeled "Orson".

A woman's voice answered, "Yes?"

"It's Maria Cartagena from social services with Sara."

A loud buzz sounded, followed by a metallic click. Maria opened the door and led Sara up the stairs to the second level. The social worker knocked on apartment number twenty-two. A short stocky woman opened the apartment door. Her haircut looked like a bowl had been put on her head and trimmed around.

"Ah, you must be Sara." She reached up slightly and put her hands on Sara's shoulders. "My, she's tall. You did say she's twelve, right?"

Maria said, "Yes. She's mature for her age. And tall."

Sara said nothing. She peeked around the woman into the apartment. In the middle of the living room, a pudgy infant stood in a playpen. He gripped the side and stared at her. Great. A baby.

"Come in, come in. I'm Mrs. Orson. Or if you want, you can call me Margie. Mr. Orson will be home in a couple of hours." Mrs. Orson let go of Sara's shoulders and stepped aside.

Sara walked in. The baby plumped down in the crib and started sucking on a blanket.

"And that's little Jacob."

Little? There was nothing little about the child. His oversized head bobbed. Sara waited for him to either fall forward or backward, but he stayed upright. Bummer.

"Can we talk, Mrs. Orson?" Maria asked.

"Sure, dear. Just let me show Sara to her room."

Mrs. Orson led Sara through the messy living room. A three-seat ratty cloth sofa faced the windows and acted as a barrier between the living room and the kitchen. Two easy chairs flanked the sofa: A brown leather one and a light tan cloth one. A credenza held a moderate-sized television that blocked half the light from the window.

"In here, dear. We have only two bedrooms. But for now, Jacob's crib is in our room."

Her own bedroom. A promising start. She'd always had to share with either another foster kid or the foster parents' own kid. Twice a baby, where she'd had little sleep.

The room contained a twin bed, neatly made, a dresser with six drawers, and a bookcase, half full of children's books. Baby stuff. On the second to last shelf sat a small statue of a man hanging from a cross, his head down. Jesus? She'd heard stories from other foster parents. Stories she'd tuned out. Kind of freaky, leaving the dude hanging there.

"Please settle in, and we'll get to know each other when Mrs. Cartagena leaves."

Oh joy. She couldn't wait. Sara placed her bag on the far side of the bed and slid it underneath halfway, then sat on the bed, waiting for Mrs. Orson. No way she'd call her Margie. She glanced at the statue.

The man on the cross raised his head and stared at her with wide open eyes. He smiled.

"Whoa." She scooted back until she reached the wall.

She closed her eyes and shook her head. No way. That didn't happen. She opened her eyes. The man's head drooped like it had been when she'd entered the room. Weird.

Getting to know Mrs. Orson consisted of learning chores she expected Sara to do. Wash and dry the dirty dishes after each meal. Empty the garbage every couple days, including the diaper pail. That one ranked at the top of favorite things she loved doing. Not. Nothing until after dinner, so she entertained herself watching not so little Jacob. She dangled a rattle above the infant's head. Jacob strained his pudgy arms, but Sara refused to let him have the toy.

The front door opened and a large man in grease-stained overalls walked in. "Who are you?" The man slipped his work boots off, leaving them by the door.

"Sara. Who are you?"

"Jim Orson. I live here."

"So do I."

"Margie, is this our foster kid?"

Mrs. Orson came out of her bedroom. "Yes, dear. This is Sara."

"Yeah, she told me that. Looks a little old. She's taller than you. Don't they age out at sixteen?"

"Eighteen, dear, is when foster kids age out. And she's only twelve."

"Really? Well, at least some more money coming in." He walked through the living room and into the bedroom. Five minutes later, he came out wearing only boxer shorts and a sleeveless T-shirt that didn't quite cover his hairy belly. He plopped into the leather easy chair.

"Make yourself useful, Sara, and get me a beer."

Sara narrowed her eyes and tried to think of a sarcastic retort. But Mrs. Orson saved her, as she breezed by and gave Mr. Orson a bottle. He grunted, twisted the top off and guzzled half of it.

This routine repeated itself daily for the next several months. Sara never got to know either Mr. or Mrs. Orson and that was fine with her. They hated her and only looked at her as a source of income. Like so many other people she knew.

*****

"Yo, Sara, what's you doing way down here, girl?"

Spike Alvarez strutted the concrete path of Dvorak Park towards Sara, who sat on a bench waiting for Jesse. The fifteen-year-old dipstick always tried putting the moves on her. As long as Jesse wasn't around. Not as tough as he pretended. And not cute at all. And if she told her homey Jesse that Spike hit on her, bye bye Spikester.

"I live over there, now." She pointed behind her. "The Orsons. You know them?"

"Got kicked out again, huh?"

She scowled at him. "Yeah. What of it?"

"Nothing, girl. You waitin 'on Jesse?"

"Yeah."

On cue, a tall, lanky milk-chocolate skinned boy appeared on the path from the ballpark. Black, silky hair brushed his shoulders as he swaggered toward them. He took long, deliberate strides. The seventeen-year-old stopped mere inches from Spike, who backed up.

"This punk givin 'you a hard time, Sara?"

"Naw. He was just walking past."

"Then keep walking, douchebag."

Spike scampered away.

Jesse sat beside her, his thigh touching hers. Butterflies swam in her belly. Always the feeling she got around Jesse until she figured out his mood. If good, then the anxiety settled into adoration.

"How'd you like that flip-phone I got you last week? It's a burner. Pretty cool, huh?"

Sara nodded and took it out. "It's great. But you're the only one I call. Don't know anyone else to call."

"That's cool. We can keep in touch. Anytime you need to talk, just ring me."

"Sure."

"So, baby-girl, how long we been together. Almost a year, isn't it?"

Eleven months and four days, but who was counting? "Yup, almost."

"And I've treated you well, right baby-girl?"

The butterflies multiplied. His soft voice caressed her as did the back of his hand on her upper arm. Unease skittered up her spine. What did he want?

"Yes, you've always treated me good." Except when he was rough with her, taking out his frustrations with his gang on her. But he always made up for it. Bought her gifts, gave her spending money, told her how beautiful she was and how much he liked her. In the entire world, only Jesse loved her. Everyone else hated her.

"I need you to do something for me."

"Sure, Jesse. Anything." Her shoulders drooped weighed down by fear. "Anything" rattled around in her mind. From Jesse, anything could be anything.

He flashed his bright white teeth and nodded. Then he put his arm around her and pulled her against him.

"There's this big dude coming from St. Louis."

"St. Louis?"

"Yeah. And this dude runs that city. He owns it. And he's looking for some partners in other cities. And this is a chance for us to hit the big time. You understand?"

She had no clue but nodded anyway.

"And this dude, he heard about you and that you and I are a thing."

"Yeah, so?"

Jesse kissed her on the forehead. "He wants to see you."

"Okay. Cool. I can meet him."

"Not just meet, baby-girl. See you. All of you."

She jerked away from him. "What do you mean all of me?"

His smile disappeared. Her butterflies turned into a flock of birds frantically trying to flee her stomach.

"No big deal, Sara. I mean look at what you did with that Garcia freak. This is only a show. You know. Show him what you got."

"I . . . I don't get it. Why me?"

His voice rose. "I didn't ask him that. He's a big dude. Important. Don't you love me? Why won't you help me out?"

"I . . . I will. I'll help you out. Sorry." She swiped the back of a hand across her eyes. No tears. Sara Hanley didn't cry.

He slid over next to her and put his arm around her again. "That's my baby-girl. And don't worry, he won't touch you or anything. And if he does, yell out, and I'll come and rescue you. Got it, baby-girl?"

"When?"

"Tomorrow. My place. Right after school."

The next day, Sara sat on a bed in one of the bedrooms of the house Jesse rented. She wrapped her arms around herself, trying to control the shivering. The door opened. A dark man filled the door. Not a speck of light filtered past him. He entered and closed the door behind him. He introduced himself as Big Eddie. When he touched her, she screamed. No one came. When he left, she curled into a fetal position and sobbed. Where had Jesse been? The things that big man did to her stabbed at her consciousness. Bile rose in her throat. She swallowed it down, not wanting to vomit all over herself or Jesse's bed.

Later, Jesse came in and sat by her. He stroked her shoulders and back and apologized many times. He explained to her that he'd heard her screams and tried to help her, but Big Eddie's goons had restrained him. The words soothed her pain. The back rub chased away the gross images. She fell asleep comforted that Jesse still loved her.

The next day, Jesse bought her some new clothes, new designer shoes, and a cool backpack for school. She shoved the experience with Big Eddie into that deep dark box where she kept all the memories of pain, focusing on ensuring Jesse's happiness so he'd continue to love her.

Big Eddie went back to St. Louis.

Sara hoped it was the last she'd see of him.

It wasn't.

For some reason, on Sara's thirteenth birthday, Mr. Orson decided she was old enough to have sex. With him. He drank a large amount of beer during her sham birthday party—large even for him. All the friends of the Orsons showed up to celebrate Sara's birthday. The Orsons didn't allow her to invite Jesse or any other kids she knew. The birthday party turned into a drinking party. Everyone ignored Sara. She squeezed into a corner of the sofa and watched a muted television. Once the guests finally left, she retreated to her room.

In the living room, Mr. Orson berated Mrs. Orson about the food she'd served. He didn't like the type of pizza or something. Sara tried to tune them out. She rummaged through the backpack Jesse had gotten her, looking for ear buds. Not there. Nor in her gym bag, still partially hidden under the bed. She lived out of that bag, never bothering to put anything in dressers or closets. Emergency precaution. She'd run out on families before.

Mrs. Orson yelled one final, "Fine", then stomped away, presumably to the bedroom. The house grew silent.

An hour later, Sara removed her tennis shoes and slipped under the covers. She tried to fall asleep, but Mr. Orson's snoring kept her awake. As she finally drifted into that state of almost being asleep, Mr. Orson's snoring stopped. The absence of sound jarred her back awake. Mr. Orson belched. The entire house shook when Mr. Orson slammed the footrest down on his easy chair.

Sara listened to his footsteps. They stopped outside her door. She threw her covers off and quickly put her tennis shoes back on, then lay onto her side facing the door and brought her knees up to her chest. The doorknob squeaked, then the door creaked as it slowly opened. The hall light fanned out over the floor of her room. Mr. Orson stood in the doorway for several seconds before advancing into her room.

"About time you earned your keep around here, girl."

Sara tensed. Mr. Orson advanced. She feigned sleep. He reached the bed. As he bent over, she rotated her hips slightly, then kicked out with both legs, catching him in the groin with a heel. He screamed like a little girl and collapsed to the floor. She jumped off the foot of the bed, grabbed her backpack and her gym bag, and bolted for the door. Mr. Orson grabbed her leg. Sara swung her book-laden backpack at his head. He yelped and let go. She shot through the bedroom door and ran down the hall, then through the living room. As she ran, she slipped her backpack over her shoulders. At the front door, she undid the dead bolt and twisted the lock on the doorknob.

Labored breathing and heavy footfalls followed her. She yanked the door, but it only opened a few inches. The chain. She slammed the door closed. Mr. Orson cursed at her. She slid the chain off. Orson's hand came down on her shoulder. She flung the door open and stepped behind it, then slammed it into Orson. He grunted and staggered back. She slipped between him and the door, opened the screen door and ran out of the house.

Orson came out onto the porch as she reached the sidewalk. "Where are you going, you little tramp? You'll be back. I'll be waiting."

She sprinted down the sidewalk and took a right at W 21st Street, then kept running until she couldn't run anymore. Sucking in air, she stopped and leaned on a chain link fence. Adrenaline coursed through her, along with anger, frustration, hopelessness. Now where? Now what?

A man approached her, weaving from one side of the sidewalk to the other. Great. A drunk. She trotted across the street and walked along some apartments. Being after eleven, only a few lights glimmered through drawn curtains. She had to find a place to hide and try to sleep. Tomorrow, she would search for Jesse and figure out what to do. Maybe he'd take her in.

Further down 21st street, semi-trucks rolled by. She passed a shipping company with open garage bay doors. What about slipping in there? She turned toward the building but saw two men deeper inside the garage. Nope. Not doing that.

One of them turned toward her. "Hey, baby. Looking for some fun?"

She trotted past the garages and kept going west until she spotted an alley on her left. At the end of the alley, she came to a gray house on the corner with a wrought-iron fence. She turned the corner and hunched down behind the fence. Through a front bay window, she saw a young man in a wheelchair and a woman standing beside him. They looked harmless. Staying hunched down, she scooted to the far corner and tossed her bag over the fence. She climbed over, careful not to cut herself on the sharp points, and sidled alongside the house until far enough not to be easily seen from the street. The adrenaline wore off. She slumped against the house and slid onto the ground. A heavy fatigue pressed against her. She started shaking, both from the cool night air and fear. From her gym bag, she pulled out a sweatshirt and draped it over herself.

After twenty minutes, the shaking eased. Her head drooped forward, and she fell asleep. Weird dreams, occasional noises, and aches in her neck woke her on and off all night, but each time, she managed to go back to sleep.

The rattle and banging of a garbage truck startled her awake. Dawn light crept toward her. She jumped up, put on the sweatshirt, grabbed her bag and backpack, and headed toward the street. No sign of the people that lived in the house. She climbed over the fence and walked toward Jesse's neighborhood, safe to walk through during the day, hoping he'd take her in.

*****

Sara approached the run-down brown brick building, indistinguishable from all the other duplexes in the neighborhood. Two boys, probably sixteen or seventeen, wearing long, baggy shorts, which they constantly pulled up, and concert T-shirts hung out at the bottom of the steps. Both also wore untied Nike high-tops with a logo of a man going for a slam dunk. She didn't know them, had never seen them.

"Hey, little girl. What's you doing here?"

"Little, Jorge? She's taller than you, dude."

"Yeah, well she's almost as tall as you, too."

"Maybe. How old are you, girl?"

"Ain't none of your business."

The shorter boy, who had a buzz cut, moved around behind her. "She sure is pretty, no matter what her age."

The taller boy moved closer to her. Sara dropped her bag and assumed a fighting stance. She figured she could kick the taller one in the groin, then run up the stairs, gaining an advantage. Someone exited the house.

"Which one of you morons wants to get slit from the throat to the crotch first?"

It was Jesse. He held a switchblade up in front of his face and grinned.

Both boys moved away from her.

"Oh, hey, Jesse," the taller one said. "You know this girl?"

Jesse sauntered down the steps. Snick. The blade disappeared into the handle. He slid the knife in his pocket. "This is Sara."

"Oh, wow, Jesse. Man, we didn't know. Never met her. Sorry.

"Get out of here." He waved them away. Both boys loped in the direction Sara had come from.

"What's you doing here, Sara?" Jesse approached her. He rubbed the back of his hand on her cheek.

"I left."

"Left what?"

"My foster family. And I ain't going back. Done with the foster scene."

Jesse slipped his arm around Sara's shoulders. "Good for you, baby. Good for you." He led her up the stairs. "Where you gonna stay?"

They stopped on the porch outside the wooden door, badly in need of stain. "I was hoping here."

"You got some money, baby? Gotta pay rent."

She shrugged out from under his arm. "You'd make me pay rent?"

"Sorry, baby. Got to. This building is owned by a dude in the Latin Kings. No one stays for free."

"I got money."

"That's good." Jesse opened the door and ushered Sara in.

They climbed more stairs to a second-floor door. He pushed it open. Dirty dishes filled half the sink. Pizza boxes littered the floor, the small round table, and the counter. Dirty glasses and plastic cups filled the remaining space.

"Maybe you can work for part of your rent. Keep the place cleaned up."

"Yeah, sure."

They left the kitchen. In the living room, four mattresses covered most of the worn, dark carpet. A teenage boy lay on one. Long black hair, bloodshot eyes. He glanced at them, then buried his head in his arm.

"He paying rent?"

"Sure. Not always in cash. Sometimes with a commodity, if you know what I mean?"

"Commodity? Not sure what you mean, Jesse."

He leaned in and whispered. "Drugs."

"Oh."

"How you feeling, baby?"

"A little lost. Frustrated. Depressed, I guess. Why?"

Jesse picked up a smoldering cigarette, only it wasn't a cigarette. It had a sweet, chemical smell. "Take a hit. This will perk you up. Might need that energy to clean this dump."

She shook her head.

"Okay, baby. Maybe later."

He showed her to a room that had a queen-sized mattress but no boxsprings.

"You can stay here. I'll keep the other dudes out of this room. Though, I might visit you once in a while. If that's okay with you."

She slowly nodded and threw her bag in the corner. Jesse left, and Sara put her backpack between the mattress and the window. She pulled up on the window. It opened. No screen. She leaned out. Only about ten feet to the ground. She could jump that, if needed. And she feared she might have to. But for now, she felt not exactly safe, but not in danger either. Jesse would protect her while he was there. But how often was he gone? And who were the other dudes who lived here? Hopefully, not the two losers who'd been hanging around outside. At least they seemed to fear Jesse. She plopped onto the mattress. Now what?

Chapter 6

"How much money do you have left?" Jesse asked Sara.

They were in her room, which she now shared with a dark-haired, slightly older girl, maybe fifteen, named Britney. The girls slept back-to-back on the lumpy mattress. Constantly high, Britney smoked meth and injected something else. Sara wondered how she paid for all the drugs.

"Nothing, Jesse. I gave it all to you."

"Then we got an issue. I can't give you hits for nothing, baby. And the rent. Gotta pay that."

"But I work for the rent."

"Part of the rent. This place ain't free, and the stuff ain't free. You know that."

She hung her head. "Yeah, I know."

Jesse put his arm over her shoulder. "Maybe you need to find a job, girl."

"I'm only thirteen. No one will hire me. I don't even have ID."

"We could fix that. Or we could find you a job that don't require an ID."

"Like what?"

Jesse maneuvered her to the bed and sat her down. She wondered if he was going to do something with her. He hadn't visited her in the room for some time. Not since he'd turned eighteen or since Britney had moved in. Though that girl was rarely around. She usually crawled into bed about five or six in the morning, then slept until mid-afternoon. During the afternoon and night, she'd fly into the bedroom, grab some stuff, and take a shower. She took five or more showers a day. Strange.

Jesse sat next to her. "You remember Big Eddie?"

Sara shuddered. She'd tried to forget Big Eddie, but she nodded.

"He was very impressed with you."

She scowled. "I don't understand. Impressed why?"

"You, girl. Just you. He said you'd be a great addition."

"To   what?"

"His business. And I've agreed to work with him. Britney is working for me. And maybe it's time you did as well. You'd be great, baby. You could bring in so much money."

Confusion clouded her brain. Spiders crawled up her spine. She wasn't sure what Jesse meant, but she didn't think she'd like it.

"I . . . I don't know, Jesse. Maybe I should just leave. That way you don't have to worry about me."

He rubbed his finger over the jade bracelet she wore. A gift from him on his birthday. She'd thought it strange that he'd given her a gift on his birthday, but he'd said he was so happy she was around.

"Where would you go? You don't want to live on the street. Bad place for a girl like you."

"What do you mean like me?"

"Beautiful. Young. I can't protect you if you take off. You gonna go back to the foster home?"

Not the one she ran from. She wondered if Maria Cartagena would help her find a new foster home. And would that be any better. She wouldn't age out of foster care for four more years.

"I don't know, Jesse. I just don't know. What is it you want me to do?"

"Same thing Britney does. Make men with money happy."

A lump formed in her throat. Her belly swam with eels. Jesse wanted her to do with others what he'd forced her to do with Big Eddie. Sex wasn't that big of a deal to her, but she didn't want to do it with random strangers.

"I don't know. I'm not sure I want to do that."

Jesse frowned. His eyes lit and Sara worried that he'd explode. He took a deep breath.

"Tell you what, take a couple days and think about it. Maybe talk to Britney. It ain't so bad, baby. And I'll make sure nothing gets out of hand." He pulled out his switchblade and flicked it open. "No one will hurt you. If they do, they'll deal with me."

He left the room. Sara fell back onto the bed and stared at the cracked ceiling. If not with Jesse, where would she go? No one else wanted her. No one else treated her well. Jesse had taken her in. He'd treated her well. Would it be that bad to do what he asked?

An hour later, Britney breezed into the room smoking something. It didn't smell as sweet as meth. Not much smell at all.

Sara sat up.

"Here you go." Britney handed Sara the joint. "Take a hit. It will help."

Sara took a deep draw, let the smoke linger, then blew it out. When she laid down, a surge of pleasure shot through her body. Heat blanketed her and she felt like she couldn't lift her arms or legs, but she didn't care. She allowed the sensation to swirl around in her until she fell asleep.

*****

The old man—a dude with greasy black hair, three-day stubble, and spindly arms—left the room. Sara figured the guy had to be at least forty. While he'd been doing his thing, she'd had the oddest out of body experience. She'd felt nothing, just floated away.

Four days ago, she'd tried the stuff Britney had offered her. Britney had told her it would help her deal with the humiliation, the feelings of being used, not viewed as a person. That morning, before the old dude entered the room, she'd finished half a smoke. Still unsure what it was. Britney called it smack. It made her feel nothing. And with that dude, it had helped her to fade away and not be present during what he'd done to her.

She slipped on an old terry cloth robe and went to the bathroom. The hot water felt great, but the more she scrubbed, the dirtier she felt. Soap didn't help. She swore she could still smell the stale cologne from that old guy. After fifteen minutes, her skin felt raw from scrubbing. She got out, dried off on a stained towel, slipped the robe back on, and left the bathroom.

In her bedroom, Sara dressed in a clean T-shirt and jeans with holes in the knees. The door burst open. Jesse stood in the doorway, hands on his hips.

"What do you think you're doing?" Jesse took two strides and stood inches from her.

"What do you mean, Jesse?"

"What was that shower? Fifteen minutes? You think water is free?"

"I'm . . . I'm sorry. I was dirty. I—"

Jesse stabbed a finger at her chest, pushing her back. "Two minutes, girl. Between customers, two minutes. Got it?"

Sara nodded.

Jesse left the room.

"Between customers" rolled around in her head like BB's in a tin can. Bile rose in her throat. She swallowed it down and searched out another joint of smack. A half-smoked one sat on Britney's nightstand next to a lighter. With trembling fingers, Sara managed to light it and inhaled. Fear and anxiety melted away as she drifted to no-feelings land.

Somewhere through the fog in her brain, Sara remembered it was Saturday evening. One more customer and she'd be done for about thirty-six hours. She pushed the plunger, then unwrapped the tourniquet and fell back onto the bed, staring at the spinning ceiling. A sense of euphoria came over her. Nothing mattered. She didn't care.

"Five minutes." Jesse stuck his head inside her room. "If you're going to shower, you better hurry." He slammed the door closed.

She hadn't showered between customers for a couple of months. Ever since she'd started injecting heroin. What was the point? She breathed in and out, in and out. Her body felt like it floated above the mattress.

The bedroom door opened again. Britney walked in.

"Come on, girl." Britney pulled Sara's arms until she got Sara into a sitting position. "You know the drill. Hey, it's the last one."

"Last one." Sara thought she stood up. At least her perspective changed to a higher view.

Britney dragged her out of the shared bedroom and to the room where she'd meet her last customer of the night. The fifth one that day. Math wasn't easy in her state, but she thought that meant about fifty bucks would come her way. She'd have to give nearly all back for rent, food, water, whatever.

Britney shoved her into the room and closed the door. Sara stumbled to the bed and sat on it. In the corner of the room stood a man in a white robe, full beard, long hair and a smile. An aura of light surrounded the man. She closed her eyes and shook her head. Still there. He remained in the corner and mouthed some words. In her head she heard, "I'm coming for you." She blinked. No man in the corner.

The bedroom door opened and in walked a short, paunchy guy with a scruffy beard who smelled like a school locker room.

*****

The sun warmed Sara to the point where she started sweating and woke up. Britney must have opened the curtain when she got up, then left. Sara shuffled to the bathroom, did her business, then took a two-minute shower. She counted to one hundred and twenty to make sure she took no longer so Jesse wouldn't yell at her. After drying and dressing, she shuffled to the kitchen. No one around. Sunday. Everyone bolted, and everyone apparently got up earlier than she did. What time was it? After a piece of toast and some orange juice, she returned to her bedroom and grabbed her phone—the same one Jesse had given her a long time ago. How long had that been? Her memory of the past year blurred together.

A little after noon. Jeez, why hadn't anyone awakened her? She decided to check outside. If it was warm enough, she'd walk around the neighborhood and try to clear her head.

She needed only a light jacket. Good thing, because that's all she had. Sometime during the past few months someone borrowed her sweatshirt but never returned it. No clue who. During most of the winter, she'd stayed in the house with nothing warm enough to be outside when cold weather rolled through. Not that she had all that much time to go anywhere anyway.

She wandered, paying no attention to where she went. Visions swam through her head. Faces of people she thought she knew, blurred distorted faces of those she didn't want to know but who had hovered over her while using her for their pleasure. She occasionally bumped into someone, apologized and kept going. Odd, no one made anything of it. She felt glares, but not a word. They probably knew who she was and who she belonged to. And no one in the Pilsen area would dare cross Jesse. From what Britney had told Sara, his influence and power had grown stronger the past several months.

Tired, she stopped at a bench on the sidewalk and collapsed. She put her head in her hands. People passed. The clack, clack of high heels, softer, squishier sounds of thick souled shoes, the click of wingtips.

Sweet, floral, and musky odors followed the footsteps. Church goers, she figured. She sat up and stared at the ghost church. She had wandered back to her old neighborhood. More visions twisted through her brain. Foster family parents and some guy she had conned out of money. Names eluded her.

A man stood on the top step of the old, abandoned church. He looked familiar. The all-white robe outfit and red scarf tweaked her memory. An older man. Clean-shaven. Wispy white hair. He motioned to her to join him.

Just what she needed. Some creepy old guy who wanted a freebie.

The man walked inside the church. Wait a minute. That place was locked up. She'd often tried to get in and never could. When she stood, she wobbled but stayed upright. Pain crawled through her head. She'd have to get back and shoot up soon or she'd start shaking. But maybe she had time to check out the ghost church.

On the steps, Sara hesitated, swayed, then reached out and grabbed the ornate bronze door handle. Door handle? There'd never been door handles since she'd been around that neighborhood. It usually had metal plates, but the doors opened out, so they couldn't be opened. She pulled, and the door opened. Whoa.

She walked in. The door closed behind her, sounding like someone scratching their nails on a blackboard. Gloomy darkness filled the place. She blinked and reached out, touching nothing. The darkness faded. Outlines of pews in rows appeared. And at the other end stood that man. Sara felt confused, disorientated. Was she in the same place? The ghost church, that only had a front wall? No side or back walls. And no roof. Must be a bad trip. She squeezed her eyes closed and banged the side of her head with the palm of her hand. When she opened her eyes, overhead chandeliers lit the church. The man at the front knelt and looked up at a cross with Jesus nailed to it. But that cross was on the outside of the church, in the back, facing the other way. She shook her head again, but nothing changed.

The man stood, turned, and smiled. He walked up the aisle toward her. A sudden bright light blinded her, then pitch-black. She moved forward and ran into a brick wall. She backed up into the door. It swung out and she stumbled into the sunlight. The door closed. Metal plates now replaced the door handles she'd used earlier.

"Where'd you come from?"

Sara jumped and looked down to her right. A homeless man in tattered jeans and an old army jacket glared at her. Brown teeth to either side of a sizable gap. Greasy graying hair hung down both sides of his head.

"I was in there."

"You can't be in there. Them doors is locked. Always has been since I been living around her. And that's years, little girl."

Sara sidled past him and quickly traversed the two concrete steps. Before she could make her complete escape, the homeless man yelled at her.

"Little girl, you need Jesus. Look to Him for help. Ain't no one else gonna help you."

Sara ran away and didn't stop running until she made it back to Jesse's house. She collapsed on the concrete steps and sucked in air. Her heart hammered. Shaking started in her belly and spread to her entire body.

Two Hispanic teenage boys approached her.

"Hey, girl, you looking to party? You need some help?"

Sara stopped shaking and stared at them. The taller, thicker one grinned and stepped toward her.

"Yo, not a good idea. Take off homey."

The teenage boy's eyes widened. He backed up, and the two teenagers fast-walked away.

"Sara, get in here."

Sara pushed off the concrete and staggered after Jesse into the house.

"I need you to pack your things. You're going on a trip."

She followed him to her bedroom. "What? Where?"

A dark-skinned guy she'd never seen before, about Jesse's height and weight, walked into her room. He had straight black hair pulled into a ponytail.

"This is Fernando. He'll drive you."

"Where? Why?" Her shaking returned. She opened the top drawer of the three-drawer dresser and pulled out her kit.

"Naw, not now, girl." Jesse slapped the kit out of her hand. "Later. Get your stuff and go with Fernando.

Sara stared at Jesse, still shaking. "I don't understand, Jesse. Why are you making me leave? Why do you hate me so much?"

"Baby-girl, get that out of your head. I don't hate you. You're my girl. But business is business, and I can't turn down this deal."

"Yeah, not just the money." Fernando chuckled. "Ain't like you can say no to Big Eddie."

"Big Eddie?" That name sounded familiar. Where had she heard his name? Fog rolled through her brain. Why was Jesse throwing her out? Who was this Fernando dude? She felt his eyes all over her.

"Forget it." Jesse pushed her aside and grabbed the sports bag on the other side of the bed. He shoved it into her stomach.

Sara clutched it. That was all she had, anyway, other than her stash. She bent over to pick up the kit, but Jesse grabbed her shoulder, pulling her back up. He shoved her out the door.

"Get going. We can't keep Big Eddie waiting."

Fernando grabbed her arm and started pulling her toward the front of the house.

"Fernando, wait."

He stopped pulling Sara at Jesse's command.

"Yea, bro."

"Her arm better be all you touch. You got that?"

"Yeah. I got it. Drive her to St. Louis. Get the money. And bring it back."

Jesse turned away and walked down the hall.

"Jesse? Why are you sending me away?"

No reply. He turned into one of the bedrooms.

Fernando pulled Sara out the door, down the steps, and to a black SUV parked on the street. He opened the front door, took her bag, helped her in the car, grabbing a feel. After slamming the door on Sara, he opened the back passenger door and threw her bag on the seat.

For the first two hours, Sara stared out the window, trying to control her shaking. Sweat beaded on her forehead and smeared the window. As they drove south, the setting sun warmed her face even more than her body was doing on its own.

"I think I'm gonna puke." She straightened in her seat.

"Not in my car, you ain't." Fernando swerved onto the shoulder of the interstate.

Sara opened the door and banged it on the guardrail. She leaned out and puked. When she was done, Fernando handed her a bottle of water. Then he opened the center console and pulled out a metal box. He opened the box and handed her a needle and a rubber tourniquet.

She shot up. The shaking stopped. She closed her eyes, and when she opened them, city lights twinkled in the darkness.

"Where . . . are we?"

"St. Louis, girl. Almost there."

They passed big, fancy houses on one side and a well-lit park on the other side. Concrete paths, large trees, people walking and jogging. She wondered if one of the big houses was their destination.

Fernando turned left into the park. He followed a winding road for a bit, then pulled into a nearly empty parking lot, where he parked in a dark corner. He shut off the car.

"Before I turn you over to Big Eddie, how about you and me have a go?"

"What?" Sara scooted as far against the passenger door as she could. "Stay away from me."

"Ah, come on. I'll be nicer than the paid customers. He reached for her, grabbed the front of her T-shirt, and pulled her toward him.

Sara chopped at his hand, knocking his grip off the T-shirt. She grabbed the door handle and rattled it. The door remained closed. "Leave me alone. I'll tell Jesse."

Fernando laughed. "Yeah, right. Like you'll ever talk to Jesse again." He lunged for her and grabbed her with both hands, pulling her close to him.

Sara struggled, shaking herself back and forth. She grabbed both his arms and dug her nails into them.

"Ouch." He yelled a profanity at her, then slapped her face. He started to grab her again, but something hard knocked against the driver's door window.

A tall, muscular man stood outside the car. He had a gun in his hand, pointing above him. "Open the door."

Fernando pulled his own gun out and laid it on his lap. He started the SUV, then rolled down the window. "What do you want, man?"

Sara noticed movement. She swiveled her head. Another man, just as tall and as big, now stood on her side of the car. He tried the door handle.

The man on Fernando's side addressed her. "You Sara?"

She nodded.

"He trying to hurt you?"

She nodded again.

"I wasn't going to hurt her. Just wanted a parting gift. You get it, don't you?"

The large man slammed Fernando in the face with his non-gun hand. Fernando fell back. His gun slipped onto the floor. Sara unlocked her door. The man outside opened the passenger door and pulled her out. Fernando leaned down to get his gun. The man on his side stuck his gun through the window.

"I wouldn't come up with that gun, if I were you."

The other man put his left arm around Sara, holding her tight to him, and pointed his gun. Fernando looked both ways, then straightened without his weapon.

"Did he hurt you? Did he do anything to you?"

Sara shook her head. Fear froze any words in her mouth. These guys were big, armed, and didn't look like anyone to mess with.

The man on Fernando's side shoved his gun against Fernando's head. "You're a lucky man. No one messes with Big Eddie's property. You got that?"

Fernando nodded. "How . . . how did you know?"

"We been watching for your vehicle. You drove right by Big Eddie's. And we saw where you turned in. Didn't take long to find you." He waggled his gun back and forth. "Now, get lost."

"The money. What about the money?" Fernando looked at one man, then the other, his eyes wide. "I'm supposed to collect and take it back to Jesse."

The man on Fernando's side withdrew his arm. "I guess you'll have to explain to Jesse what happened. You got ten seconds to go, or I start shooting."

The man who held Sara closed the passenger-side door.

Fernando shifted the vehicle into reverse and backed up, then drove away.

"Come on, let's get you to Big Eddie." The man who had been on Fernando's side walked up to her. "I'm Jerome. And that's Maurice. There ain't nothing to be afraid of. Big Eddie will take care of you."

The violent shaking that wracked Sara's body was not from withdrawal. Not this time.

Maurice helped Sara out of the SUV. Jerome led them around the back of the massive three-story, light-brown brick house. There were spotlights on the front and the side they walked on. Another massive man stood on the porch outside the front door.

When they reached the back, Sara smelled chlorine. They climbed three stairs that led to a deck. Out beyond an iron gate, water glimmered in the full moonlight. A pool? Jerome opened one half of a double-door and waved her in. She entered a brightly lit kitchen. A brick oven was recessed into the opposite wall. On both sides of the double door were large bay windows with sitting ledges. All the walls were white. White pots and pans hung from large hooks in the white ceiling over a white granite-covered island. To her right, six padded chairs surrounded a white ceramic-topped table with a blonde wood frame.

Jerome led them left, out of the kitchen and into a family room. Two armchairs and a couple of sofas, all clean, white, leather. Jerome motioned for her to sit. She perched on the edge of one of the sofas.

"Thank you, Jerome, Maurice. You can leave us now."

Sara swiveled her head and the giant man she'd met a couple years ago, Big Eddie, walked into the family room. A huge smile decorated his face with bright, even teeth. His eyes sparkled. He wore a white button-down shirt and off-white pants. His dark, bare feet in the white, plush carpet looked like bear cubs laying in snow.

"Good evening, Sara. Do you remember me?" His voice boomed.

She lowered her head, clasped her hands together in her lap, and nodded.

"No need to be afraid, young lady. You will be treated well here." Big Eddie sat on the cushion next to hers. He patted her shoulder. "For tonight, you'll stay here. We have a room ready for you. Tomorrow, Tanya will help you move into her apartment. She lives above the place where you'll be working. There are two bedrooms."

Sara brought her shaking under control. She glanced at Big Eddie. The man still smiled. He seemed genuinely nice. His eyes never wavered from her eyes. She could not detect any malice in them. Thinking back to the first time they'd met, she realized, despite the shameful things he'd done to her, he'd been gentle. Never raised his voice or hurt her.

"What kind of work?"

He chuckled. "Nothing different from what you've been doing. Servicing customers. But the clientele will be a little better class, I believe."

"Clientele?"

"Your customers."

"Where will I be working?"

"At a massage parlor I own in the Central West End. Nice place. Classy. The masseuses are all friendly."

Massage parlor? "I don't know anything about massaging people."

He chuckled again. "Don't worry. That's not what you'll be doing. You'll stay in one of the other rooms. The masseuses will send you your customers. I promise, you'll have at least thirty minutes between each one."

"Oh." She latched onto that one positive thing. Thirty minutes between degradations.

A thin, white woman walked into the family room.

"Ah, Margarite, please show Sara to her room for tonight." Big Eddie stood. "You can sleep in tomorrow. Margarite will take good care of you. You'll start work on Monday. The parlor is closed on Sundays." He walked out of the room.

Sara looked up at Margarite. Her shaking started again. "I . . . I need something—"

"Yeah, honey. I know what you need. Follow me."

Sara followed Margarite down a hallway and up a flight of stairs to what she woman referred to as a small bedroom. Small? What did they consider large? Margarite showed Sara around the room. In a walk-in closet Margarite told her to select any clothes she wanted. All were her size. All were brand new. Margarite left saying she'd be back shortly.

Sara sat on the bed. So soft. She bounced and wished she could stay there. Margarite returned and handed Sara a tourniquet and a needle ready to inject. Which she did. She breathed deeply, then fell back on the bed. The older woman removed the tourniquet and switched off the light on her way out of the room.

Sara scooted up into the bed, not bothering to undress or pull down the covers. She studied the murky ceiling above her. Suddenly, a face hovered above hers. A bearded man. In her mind she heard the words, "You're here."

She closed her eyes, opened them. No more vision. Minutes later, she drifted off into bliss.

*****

Time passed. Days became weeks, which became months. The massage parlor worked no differently from Jesse's house, except Sara was given ten minutes to shower between customers. But she didn't get Sundays off. Big Eddie had told her the massage parlor closed on Sundays. It did, but only for the masseuses. Not for her.

She hadn't been to Big Eddie's since that first night. The bed she slept in had a thin mattress, but by the time she fell asleep, she didn't care or notice, drifting away into heroin bliss. Besides the bed, her bedroom upstairs had a two-drawer dresser with a couple changes of clothing, and a rickety nightstand with one drawer that housed her paraphernalia.

On a day that morning sleet turned to afternoon rain, after her last customer, a large smelly man with wispy hair and three-day stubble left, Sara put on her fake silk robe and slipped into her flip flops. She started for the shower when the door opened. A wiry black man about her height walked   in.   She'd   never   seen   him   before.

"Who are you? I don't have any more customers."

The man walked straight at her and grabbed her arm. "Let's go. You're coming with me."

Sara jerked her arm out of his grip. He backhanded her across the face. She staggered and rubbed her cheek.

"Let's go." He opened the door and stood half in the room and half in the hall.

Sara looked at the floor. "Can I get dressed first?" He must be someone who worked for Big Eddie. Best not to make him any more angry.

"Yeah. But hurry up."

She edged past him, climbed the stairs, and went to her room. He followed her. She closed the door on him. There was no lock. The man opened her door and again stood half in her room and half in the hall. He watched her remove her robe and put on her clothes. Jeans and the one sweater she owned. It was dark blue with a high collar. Not real heavy, but good enough. She grabbed her ski jacket—a present from Cora, the owner of the parlor—and slipped it on.

The man stepped into her room and again grabbed her arm. She had to walk fast to keep up, pretty sure if she fell, he'd just drag her. They went downstairs. Before he pulled her out the door, Cora, a thick woman in her forties with long black hair, waved to her. Sara waved back, wondering if she'd ever see the owner again.

A beefy black man and a thinner white man with a crewcut waited outside. Each took one arm and led her to a white SUV. The man who'd brought her downstairs opened the back driver's side door and the other two helped her in.

"Where   are   we   going?"   Sara   asked.

Someone slammed the door shut. The men piled into the SUV.

"We'll start her at the club in East St. Louis," the man who'd grabbed her said. "See how she works out."

"Okay, boss." The other black man drove.

Sara crumpled against the car door. She wrapped her arms tightly around her chest and stared out the window at the cold, dreary fading daylight.

By the time they drove across the bridge, darkness had enveloped the city. The tall, well-lit buildings of the city disappeared. The SUV dodged in and out of traffic on the highway, then took an exit for East St. Louis. They pulled into the parking lot of a small building with no windows and no sign.

They walked her inside. Blaring rock music and flashing colored lights assaulted her. She winced and covered her ears. They continued past a figure eight stage. On it were three poles from floor to ceiling. And on all three poles, women wearing almost nothing swung, climbed, and gyrated. Television screens on the wall showed other dancing women. Men occupied tables scattered around the rest of the room. At most tables, a woman dressed similar to the pole dancers sat on their laps.

The white guy opened a back door, and she was shoved through. The man who'd pulled her out of her room followed her. He shut the door, leaving the other two men outside the office.

"Sit." He pointed to a vinyl chair in front of a desk, then sat in the chair behind the desk.

She sat and put her head in her hands.

"Look at me."

She did.

"My name is Keyshawn Williams. As of right now, I own you. This is my club. You ever dance?"

Sara shook her head. Behind Keyshawn hung a calendar with a bikini-clad woman leaning over a classic car. The rest of the office consisted of a fake plant and a filing cabinet.

"Wait tables?"

She again shook her head.

"Can you learn anything?"

She nodded.

"Good." He picked up a desk phone and punched a button. After a few seconds, he said, "Send Marlene in." He put the phone down and stared at her. "How old are you?"

"Sixteen."

He sighed, shoved his lower jaw out, chewing on his upper lip.

A knock on the door.

"Come in."

A blonde woman entered, wearing a silky robe with her hair stacked on her head. "Roland said you wanted me."

Keyshawn stood. "Marlene, meet Sara. Sara, meet Marlene. Go with her. Do what she says, and there won't be no trouble."

Marlene put her hands on her hips and glared at Keyshawn. "What do you want me to do with her? She can't do tables. Not old enough. You want her on a pole?"

"How do you know how old she is?"

"Don't take no rocket scientist to see she's under twenty-one. Ain't been too used up, yet."

"No pole. Backroom." Keyshawn waved his hand, shooing them out.

Marlene grabbed Sara's hand. "Come on, honey."

Sara stood and followed Marlene through the club and through another door on the far side of the stage. They continued down a hallway lined with four doors, two on each side. Three were closed. Marlene led her to the far-left door, revealing a small room with nothing but a twin bed and a splotched wooden nightstand on the far side of the bed. Overhead, fluorescent lights crackled. The place smelled moldy.

"Home sweet home, baby. Be here by noon. And you can leave at two AM during the week and four AM on weekends." She pulled Sara back into the hall. "That door at the end leads to a couple showers. On a busy night, the customer gets fifteen. Then you get five to shower. Get what I'm saying?"

Sara nodded.

Marlene shoved her back into the room. "If you ain't with a customer or showering, stay here until you're free to leave." She moved toward the door.

"Can I ask you something?"

Marlene stopped. "Sure, honey. Anything."

"Where do I go?"

Marlene flashed a wry grin. "Honey, that ain't my problem. Just be back by noon tomorrow."

Sara frowned, trying to think through the haze of her withdrawal. Her stomach hurt.

"You got something else to ask?"

"My stuff back at the parlor. Will someone bring it?"

"No. Everything you need is in that drawer." She pointed to the nightstand.

"Clothes?"

"You're wearing them, honey. Anything else is up to you." Marlene walked out the door and slammed it shut.

Sara walked to the nightstand and opened the drawer. Paraphernalia similar to her nightstand at the parlor rested inside, but only two packets. How would that get her through twenty-four hours? She flopped onto the bed as questions steamrolled through her head. Where would she go in the morning? What would she eat? Drink? Do until noon tomorrow? She pulled the stuff out of the drawer.

As she put the paraphernalia back, the door opened and a thirtyish man in a gray pin-striped suit entered.

[section break]

Sara lay back on the bed, hoping that was the last customer. She let her mind wander back to Chicago. Walking in a park, sun shining, a soft breeze caressing her cheek. Her mother walked beside her, holding her hand, laughing, telling her how beautiful she was. She started to drift, soar above that park, her arms out like an eagle, the wind carrying her away out of the filthy city into a countryside she could only imagine.

Her door opened.

Sara crashed to reality. But it wasn't a man.

The young blonde woman smiled. Buxom, tall, like Sara, but broader. Not overweight. Well-proportioned. She wore a short tight brown skirt and cream-colored Henley shirt with all three buttons undone. "Hi. I'm Candy. It's almost Christmas, so my last name for a couple months is Kane. Get it? Candy Kane?"

Sara sat up and nodded. "Just Sara."

Candy approached the bed and shook Sara's hand. "No last name?"

"Hanley. Nothing as exciting as yours." Sara tried to smile, but mirth had fled from her months ago.

Candy stroked her cheek. "So young. Anyway, Big Eddie sent me. Come with me, and I'll take you to where you can stay." She moved back to the wall by the door.

Marlene flashed in. "You still here? Get out."

Candy cleared her throat.

Marlene glanced to her left. "Oh, Ms. Kane. Sorry, I didn't know you were here." Marlene left the room.

"Wow." Sara's eyes widened. "She seemed afraid of you."

Candy smiled again and shook her head. "Not of me. Of Big Eddie. I'm one of his girls."

She walked back to the bed and put her hand out. Sara took it. Candy pulled her out of the bed and through the nearly empty club. In the parking lot, she opened the door of a small sports car with an infinity symbol on the trunk.

Sara sat in the passenger seat.

Candy got in the driver's side. "No one messes with Big Eddie's girls." She winked at Sara.

Fifteen minutes later, Candy led Sara to an apartment. Simple. One bedroom. A small kitchenette and living area. A small television sat on a worn credenza. Inside a half-sized refrigerator, Candy showed Sara some TV dinners and soda cans. In one cabinet she showed Sara a box of cereal, a box of rice, and a couple cans of vegetables.

"Enough to get you started. Keyshawn will pay you at the end of each week. It isn't that much, but if you limit your drug use, you won't starve."

Limit her drug use? And have to face reality? Sara wasn't sure that would be possible. But maybe with Candy's help, she'd try.

"Thank you."

Candy nodded and left. That was the only time Sara ever saw her.

The months passed. The seasons changed. Sara only noticed because of the clothing she had to wear to get to the club. The rest of her days she spent in the tiny room in the hall in the back of the club.

Bored one night, she wandered into the club between customers.

Marlene saw her and dragged her back to her room. She slugged Sara in the stomach. "Did you forget? Stay here." She left.

Sara bent over on the bed, willing herself not to puke. As soon as she could straighten, she used the last packet she had for that day, unless she asked for more and had more money docked from her meager pay. She fell back onto the bed and waited.

An hour went by. Then two. No one entered the room. Time dragged. She paced. After waiting about four hours, she opened her door and peaked out. A man came in the door at the end of the hallway, led by one of the dancers. But she ushered him into a room on the other side of the hall, shut the door and returned to the main area.

Another two hours went by. The tiny digital clock on her nightstand crept along until two a.m. arrived. No one had come to her the entire day. She left her room. In the main club she hesitated. The two bouncers and Keyshawn talked at the bar. He looked at her then gestured her over to them. Her stomach rumbled and cramped. Hunger and fear, a bad combination.

"Don't bother coming here tomorrow." Keyshawn looked at the buzz-cut white guy. "Take her to where I told you. Just after dark. Got it."

The white guy nodded. "You got a ride home?"

Sara looked around.

"Honey left," Keyshawn said.

Sara shook her head.

The white guy grabbed her arm. "Okay. Let's go. I need to know where to get you, anyway."

Neither one spoke on the ride to her apartment. He parked in the lot, got out and opened her door for her. She thought he was being a gentleman. Forty minutes later, when he left her apartment, she knew he wasn't any kind of gentleman.

*****

At least Keyshawn had waited until warmer weather to throw her out on the street. The dress code changed. At the club, it didn't matter what she wore, as it wasn't on her that long. She usually wore a robe between customers. On the street, she had to be a billboard, advertise herself. Being tall and well-arranged, as one older man had told her, opened up many options to display herself. But she hated it. Hated the tiny skirts, the tight, revealing tops, the high heels. Hiding her needle tracks sucked. Injecting between her toes hurt. Walking all night on those same toes produced excruciating pain. And some nights, that's all she did. And on those nights, she ate little and missed her only relief. The days following those nights lasted an eternity. Unable to sleep, sweats alternated with chills. Nauseated with a pounding headache. She usually ended up on the couch watching daytime television, dreaming of home, of times with her mother before all the men. She knew the dreams were fantasies. She'd been two when her mother gave her up.

And she hated talking to potential customers, but Keyshawn seemed to have a radar. The only nights he patrolled to check on his girls were the nights she tried to slack off by hanging back, leaning on one of the buildings. Keyshawn always caught her. He knew how to hit her, so it didn't leave a mark but still hurt for several days.

Her last night on the street started quietly. No Keyshawn yet. No other girls within two blocks. It was a warm, late September night, and she wore white short-shorts, fishnet stockings, a black half-top, and black three-inch heels. She detested the heels. Her ankles wobbled when she walked. She confined her pacing to two sidewalk rectangles, pretending the lines were electrified fences, not crossing them.

A limo pulled to the curb. The back passenger side window descended. She sighed, then smiled and walked to the car.

49

"Hey, baby, looking for some fun." She purposely raised her voice timbre, sashayed her hips some and leaned over to give the older man in the back of the limo a good view.

The man's gaze stayed locked on her face. The door opened. The man slid over to give her room. She climbed in and sat on the soft leather seat, then scooted close to the man. He had gray-flecked brown hair combed in a side part, a goatee also flecked with gray, a warm smile and brown, bright eyes. His gaze stayed on her face. Sara placed one hand on the inside of his thigh and the other around his neck. She frowned when he pushed both of her hands away.

"Drive."

When he spoke the command, she looked forward and noticed a black man in the driver's seat. Shaved head. Thick neck.

"What's your name?" the man asked.

Another thing she hated, making up names that were evocative. "Pleasure."

"Your real name?"

She frowned. His gaze stayed locked on her face and his smile frozen. She felt it to be genuine, compassionate. Warmth radiated off the man. Still, she had a job to do and wanted to eat the next day and relieve the headache starting to form.

"Hey, I want my money up front. You're creeping me out." Not really, but she felt it needed to be said to get things rolling. She glanced out the window. Buildings flashed by. They passed the entrance to a parking lot. "Where are we going?" She'd forgotten to direct them to go to the parking lot four blocks from where she walked. That was the usual spot. The man's kind face had distracted her.

The man smiled again. "Somewhere safe." He extracted a wallet from inside his sports jacket, opened it, and handed her a one-hundred-dollar bill. "Will that suffice?'

She flashed a seductive smile. "Sure. Now, what can I do for you? Nothing too kinky, though." Weird. She felt almost dirty saying that to this man. What was his deal?

"Tell me your real name."

That was a no-no, but for some reason, she felt compelled to answer. "Sara. Sara Hanley." Getting back into her role, she affected a heavy Southern twang. "I'm from Birmingham. Nice to meet you, suh. What's your name?" Again, she felt a wave of guilt lying to him like that. But she smiled big and stuck out her hand.

"Calvin Rockport. Nice to meet you, Sara."

The limo entered the freeway, busy on a Friday night.

She frowned. "Where are we going?"

"My place. You'll like it. I live in Huntleigh Woods."

She hoped he'd be paying her more as it would definitely be longer than an hour. And if she came up short, Keyshawn would take it out of her in flesh.

She smiled, showing all her white teeth. "Wow! And what are we going to do there?" She didn't think they were cops, especially since he'd given her money and she hadn't said she'd do anything. However, she couldn't be too careful. The first time in jail still haunted her, even though it lasted only over the weekend.

"Be patient. You'll find out."

"Like I said, nothing too kinky. I'm not into that stuff."

"Don't worry, nothing like that."

They rode in silence for the next fifteen minutes. She felt his eyes on her continually. She feigned indifference and looked out the window, then back at him. Something in his look felt different. Not the usual lust. A deep sadness. A half-smile stayed pasted on his face as his eyes drifted in and out of a faraway look. She wanted to know what thoughts swirled around in that rich brain of his.

On Interstate 40, traffic streamed by. The intermittent flashes of headlights strobed the inside of the limo. With each flash, she caught his soft, caring gaze. Something was so off with this guy as far as her usual customer. What did he truly want? What would he make her do?

"We're here," the driver said, as they pulled into a long semi-circular, well-lit driveway and stopped alongside a two-story, mostly stone house with an A-frame gabled roof.

"Whoa. This is yours?" Sara asked.

Rockport nodded. The driver came around and opened the door. Rockport stepped out of the limo. He started to go around to the other side, but the driver whispered something she couldn't hear into his ear.

Rockport's answer sounded like, "Keep her."

Keep her? What did that mean? She scrunched back into the corner of her seat. Did she want to find out?

The driver replied, "But . . ."

Rockport nudged past the driver before he could finish. The older man came around the car and opened Sara's door.

She stared at him and decided she'd risk it. How much worse could anything they did to her be from what people already did to her on a regular basis? She slipped out and stood in the driveway. Two lions on pedestals framed the front stoop. That was cool. She'd love to have lion statues. A light shone through the large porthole window centered on the second floor. She leaned her head back, then side to side.

"You got a pool?" she asked.

"Yes, I do."

"Let's go skinny dipping." She skipped up the front steps and waited for Rockport. Maybe this would be fun.

The driver brushed past her and opened the door. She practically ran inside. Rockport followed. She tilted her head and pointed to the chandelier above her.

"Look at all that glass."

"Crystal, my dear. It's crystal."

"Whoa." She twirled taking in the massive foyer. The wood floor glistened in the light of the chandelier. To her left, she spotted a formal dining room. Her stomach growled. It had been hours since she'd eaten a minuscule lunch of potato chips. In front of her, the carpeted staircase made two turns to the second floor.

"This way." Rockport headed through an archway on her right.

She followed him. When they entered the room, Sara flew past him. "Whoa! So . . . clean." She darted to the middle of the room and twirled. "This place is huge. I love the zebra stripes." She sat in one of the zebra-striped chairs with brown, leather cushions. She bounced up and down a couple times and waited to be yelled at. As a kid, when she'd bounced on cheap, over-used furniture the foster parents had screamed at her.

Rockport sat on one of two white sofas, perpendicular to each other and the chairs. Three glass tables formed an "I" in the middle of the room. On the two end tables sat crystal bowls. Three crystal candles and a light blue tinted crystal statue that looked like a tree in winter decorated the bigger, middle table.

Rockport asked, "Can I get you a soda or something?"

She cocked one eyebrow at him and frowned. "Seriously? A soda? Got anything stronger?"

Rockport hesitated. "Let me look." He walked to a cabinet at the far end of the living room and bent down.

Sara leaned back, kicked off her heels and put her feet on the glass table. She tossed a yellow pillow up into the air and caught it. She launched the pillow again and caught it.

Rockport put a syringe, a spoon, a rubber tourniquet, and a small jar with crystal powder on the table closest to Sara.

"Well, well, look at this. A Franklin and some brown sugar." Sara switched to her heavy Southern accent again. "Aren't you accommodating to little ole me." She swung her legs down and batted her eyes at him, then patted the cushion next to her. "I'm sure you could squeeze in with me."

Instead, Rockport sat on the sofa, then picked up the spoon and scooped some of the powder onto it. He fished a lighter from his jacket pocket.

She carefully took the spoon from him. "I'll hold it."

Rockport flicked the lighter on and held it under the spoon. As soon as the powder was liquefied, she handed him the spoon and wrapped the tourniquet around her upper arm, then palpitated her vein in the crook of her elbow. It wasn't ideal, as it would leave a mark and Keyshawn might get mad at her, but doing it between her toes seemed awkward and a little embarrassing in front of this man. Sara picked up the syringe and sucked up most of the liquid.

"How pure?" she asked.

"Pretty good."

She injected the liquefied powder into her vein then laid back to wait for the effect. "Now, don't you be taking advantage of little ole me." She winked at him and lifted her top to expose her breasts in a black, lacy bra.

He watched her face. She smiled. Her eyes grew heavy. Something wasn't right. She frowned and tried to sit up but could not. Her eyes shut tight, and blackness engulfed her.

Sara opened her eyes. What was that above her? A dark cloth ceiling? Where was she? She turned her head. A bedroom? A really nice bedroom. The mattress she lay on was so soft. A blue blanket covered her. The bed had a pole on each corner holding the cloth ceiling. Under her was a maroon, quilted bedspread. She threw aside the blanket and realized she was still wearing her clothes, minus the spiked heels. She sat up and swung her legs over the side of the canopy bed. At least that's what she thought it was called. She'd heard about them once but never seen one, let alone been in one. Her heels sat on the floor near the bed. She slipped them on.

Against the wall to her left sat a strange wooden desk. It had two drawers on each side and an oval mirror in the middle with an ornate gold frame. A lamp with a white shade took up one corner of the desk, which she now thought wasn't really a desk, but didn't know what it was. Nothing else occupied the desk's surface. An armless, purple cloth chair sat in front of the desk. Nothing on the top of the antique nightstand near the bed. One window. Gold and maroon drawn curtains hung from the top of the window to the floor. To her right, near the closed door, sat an armchair. The color matched the bedspread but had white spots. A small round wooden table occupied the corner right of the chair. An identical lamp to the one on the desk sat on the table.

She slid forward and stood. Fuzziness rushed to her head. She grabbed one of the canopy poles to steady herself. After a deep breath, she wobbled to the door. Locked.

"Hey, is anyone out there? Hello. Open the door, will ya?" She felt the presence of someone on the other side of the door. "Hey. Let me out of here." She rattled the doorknob. "I know you're out there. Open the door."

The door opened and the older man named Rockport stepped into the room.

Sara backed away toward the canopied bed. She bumped into the nightstand. "What did you give me last night? That wasn't brown sugar." She didn't bother with her fake Southern accent.

"It was a sedative."

"What do you want with me?" She leaned to the side, looking beyond him, gauging her chances of running, but unsure where she'd run to.

"I want to help you."

"Help me? By knocking me out and locking me up?"

"I'm sorry about that. You need to stay in here a few days."

She widened her eyes. "What?"

"For your own good, you'll need to stay in here. We'll bring you food and water."

"Look, buddy, I don't know what you're into—"

"And we'll have a doctor here to help you with the withdrawal."

She charged and tried to dodge around him. He grabbed her arm. She wrenched it free, but he got his other hand around her and wrapped her in a bear hug.

"Let me go! Help! Help me!" She kicked back and down, driving her three-inch heel into his shin.

Rockport lost his grip on her. She wriggled free, then spun around and slugged him in the nose. Sara turned and ran directly into a wall made of flesh, standing six feet five, weighing over three hundred pounds.

The large man bear hugged Sara and pushed her back into the room. As he drew even with Rockport, he released one beefy arm and shoved the older man out the door. He then pushed Sara to the bed, and quicker than she could believe, darted out of the room and closed the door.

Sara shot off the bed and launched herself at the door, but the solid wood held. She shook the doorknob as hard as she could. "Let me out. You can't keep me here. Let me out!" She put her ear against the door and heard receding footsteps. "No, please come back. Let me out. You can't keep me here."

The big man who had stopped her said, "What are we going to do with her?"

Their voices faded into the distance. All she heard of Rockport's answer was, "Keep her in there until she goes through withdrawal."

Sara turned, put her back against the door, and slumped to the floor. The first shakes hit her. She wrapped her arms around her torso and shivered. Five minutes passed and the shivering stopped. She took her heels off and flung them across the room, then got up and crawled under the blanket on the bed, trying to get warm. Over the next couple hours, she fought waves of nausea, trembling, and a headache. At some point, the door opened. She glanced in that direction. A woman approached her with a syringe in one hand. The big guy walked next to her, eyeing Sara as they approached. He carried a brown bottle and some white, fluffy stuff. Sara shook and shivered, no energy to try and escape.

"This will help." The woman sat on the edge of the bed and pulled down the blanket enough to expose Sara's shoulder. The big guy took the lid off the brown bottle and put a cotton ball on the opening, then tilted the bottle up. He handed the cotton ball to the woman who wiped Sara's shoulder. Sara didn't feel the needle go in.

The woman, who appeared to be in her forties smiled at her, then rubbed Sara's hair. "You'll sleep now. Just a few days and the nausea should pass. Try eating something later. It will help." She eased off the bed.

Sara wanted to tell them to let her go home, but lack of energy and nowhere she thought of as home prevented her from speaking. The pair walked toward the bedroom door. Before they'd left the room, she fell asleep.

Over the next four days, they were the only people Sara saw. The woman with short blonde hair, who she learned was Dr. Miranda Cortez, didn't speak Spanish. She'd married a Cortez, who apparently didn't speak Spanish either. Of course, the big guy accompanied her on every trip, thus limiting her ability to escape. And when she had to go to the bathroom, they walked beside her, one on either side, each holding one of her arms as they traversed fifteen feet down the hallway.

The bathroom had a small window. Sara examined it. She could probably squeeze through, but it was a long drop to the ground. Not worth the risk, especially in a weakened state.

Each morning, lunch time, and evening, the big guy brought her a meal. Mostly bland stuff. Oatmeal, peanut butter sandwiches, rice, some fruits, and some vegetables.

Day five of her captivity, she felt better. The nausea stayed at bay. Her strength returned. No more headaches or chills. That night, she slept well and woke up with a renewed spirit. She thought hard but couldn't remember the last time she'd been sober, the last time she'd gone more than a day without the junk.

The big guy entered with a tray of food. She smelled the maple and brown sugar in the oatmeal as soon as he walked through the door. Her stomach rumbled, and her mouth watered. He put the tray on the otherwise empty nightstand. So far, the big guy had remained mute. He normally stood over her and waited for her to eat, which she did. More each day as the nausea subsided.

She flung the blanket aside. Still wearing the same clothes she'd come with, she decided it was time to get cleaned up. Then escape.

"I'd like to take a shower."

"After breakfast that can be arranged."

"He speaks." She sat up and swung her legs over the bed. The maple and brown sugar smelled wonderful. Two pieces of buttered toast and orange juice in a plastic cup accompanied the oatmeal. "What's your name?"

"Chester."

"Nice to meet you, Chester."

"Likewise. Glad to see you're feeling better. May I pray before you eat?"

That was a first. Usually, he put the tray down and retreated to the other side of the room, sat in the chair, and waited.

"Um, sure. Won't hurt, I guess."

Chester smiled. "No, it won't hurt." He bowed his head, but he didn't close his eyes. Guess he didn't trust her. She wouldn't trust her either. Sara closed her eyes and bowed her head.

"Dear Lord, thank you for this bounty and for all You provide for us. Thank you for bringing this young girl into our lives. Give us guidance and wisdom to help her leave the life. I pray for her spiritual health and that she'd become a child of Yours. In Jesus's holy and precious name. Amen."

Sara muttered, "Amen." She looked up at Chester. "Um, thank you, I guess. But what I'd really like is to go home."

Chester turned away from her and walked to the other side of the room. Rude. But he grabbed the chair and picked it up like it weighed nothing, brought it over to the side of her bed, and sat.

"And where exactly is home?"

She spooned some oatmeal into her mouth. Man, that tasted great. She took a bite of toast and washed it down with orange juice. Her taste buds had returned in full force, and her head had cleared so she could smell everything. She sighed. Where was home? Great question. Where exactly would she go? Back to the apartment? No way. That place sucked. Back to the nightclub? She'd be beaten and put back to work. Back to Chicago? Jesse would probably find her, beat her, and return her to Big Eddie. But was she even safe here? Couldn't Big Eddie still find her?

She looked at Chester who watched her. Patient man. "Um, I've never really had a home, at least not since I was a baby."

He nodded. "Wanna go?" He pointed at the open door. "Go."

Was he really letting her walk out? Last time she'd tried to escape, he'd carried her back into the room. What was his game?

"You'd let me go?"

He shrugged. "Mr. Rockport would not be pleased, but if you really have some place better to go, then go."

She ate some more oatmeal. What had they done to her? They'd fed her. Medicated her. Nursed her through withdrawal. No strange, sweaty, disgusting men came into her room and had their way with her. No one beat her if she didn't do exactly what they wanted. Sure, they'd locked her up, but maybe that had been for her own good. But what would she do here? How long would they let her sponge off them?

"Why are you doing this?" Sara asked.

"Know whose room this is?"

"No. How would I know?"

"It's Mr. Rockport's daughter's room."

Sara looked around. She'd guessed it was a girl's room, being all frilly and such. "And where's Mr. Rockport's daughter?"

"Died of a heroin overdose."

"Oh." She studied the remaining food on her tray. Not a bad way to go, just drift off into oblivion. She'd thought about it many times. Shoot up a little too much and leave this hell hole. Well, not this particular place, it didn't seem like a hell hole, but where she'd been before.

"Still didn't answer me. Why?"

Chester sighed and looked up. His lips moved. He clasped his hands together. Then he lowered his head and looked deep into Sara's eyes. "Do you wanna know why *I* do this or why *Mr. Rockport* does this?"

"Both."

Chester chuckled. "Kinda demanding, aren't you?"

Sara smiled. The sensation on her face felt odd. When was the last time she'd smiled? But something about this big man loosened her up.

She sensed and saw the respect he had for her as a person. But she also saw and felt the frustration he had with her background. "Please?"

"I'll start with Mr. Rockport. Easier for me to tell. His daughter, Carolyn, got hooked on heroin. Started small, from what I've been told. Pot, speed, some coke. Her mother had died. Mr. Rockport worked long hours. Carolyn was lonely. She ran away."

"She left all this? Did she have mental issues?"

Again, Chester chuckled, but this one carried no amusement. "Having every material thing you ever want ain't enough, girl. The one thing she really needed was love. She felt abandoned by her mother and ignored by her father."

Sara nodded. Tears formed in the corners of her eyes. They burned. What was going on? Cry? That wasn't happening. She rubbed the backs of her hands across her eyes.

"Something strike you? Sound familiar?"

"Love?" She spit the word out. "Not sure I know what that is."

"I hear ya, girl. That's how Carolyn felt. Unfortunately, she was lost. No Jesus to guide her. She got in with the wrong people. They trafficked her. She did porn. Eventually, she overdosed. We tried to find her, but we were too late."

More tears slid down Sara's temples. She shook her head. There was that Jesus thing again. What could a dead guy do for her?

"It's okay. Maybe you have some things to let go of."

"Keep going." She again tried to wipe away the tears, but they kept coming.

"Mr. Rockport wanted absolution. He was forgiven by Jesus, but he couldn't forgive himself, so he dedicated the rest of his life to helping girls so they wouldn't end up like Carolyn."

"Jesus? I don't get it."

"Do you know who Jesus is?"

She nodded, then shook her head. "I don't know. Some holy dude that died a long time ago."

Another chuckle from Chester. "Some holy dude. I like that. Understatement, but true. But not *some* holy dude. *The* holy dude. The son of God who came to earth, lived as a man, and died on the cross, taking all of our bad stuff onto Himself, so we could be forgiven by God. And then He rose from the dead."

"Ain't no god going to forgive me. I've been doing bad since I was ten."

"You and me both, girl. I killed a man in anger. Yes, Jesus forgave me. You ever kill anyone?"

Sara stared at him, a little fearful. He'd killed someone? But then she'd been around a lot of killers. And none of them had been like Chester. "And this holy dude forgave you?"

"God forgave me because of what Jesus did on the cross."

"He died. I don't get it."

"He didn't just die. He sacrificed himself in place of all of us. See, we all do bad stuff. You believe that?"

She tsked. "Of course. Haven't met anyone yet who only did good."

"Exactly. And because of that, we can't get to heaven because God doesn't want people who've done bad in His heaven."

"God must be one lonely dude."

Chester nodded. "He would have been, except for Jesus." He paused and studied his hands. "You ever been to court?"

Sara nodded.

"Were you convicted?"

"Misdemeanor. Prostitution, you know?"

"Sure. Let's say you had murdered someone, and you're found guilty, and the judge sentences you to death."

"Okay."

"And someone else comes into the courtroom and says to the judge that he'll take your punishment. That the state can execute him if they set you free."

"Why would anyone do that?"

"Because God loves us that much. We're his creation. He wants only good for us, but He also lets us make our own choices. And some of us don't make good choices."

"Like me, you mean?" She stared hard at him. But he didn't flinch, and his eyes remained soft, full of caring and concern.

"And like me, girl. I made plenty of bad choices."

"Okay, so what? Some dude says he'll die for me."

"That's Jesus. That's what He did for all of us. If we put our trust in Him, if we confess Him as the Lord of our life and allow Him to guide us, we can go to heaven because God only sees Jesus and not us. God forgets all about the bad stuff we've done."

"But I don't get it. How does He guide us now? He's dead."

"Ah, there's the great part of the good news. Three days after He was killed, He rose again, conquering death, and paving the way for us to live forever with God."

Sara thought about what Chester said, but it was too much. She couldn't wrap her mind around it. Why would anyone love her, anyway? Even God.

"Why are *you* doing this?" She wanted to get back to something she could latch onto.

"We'll talk about Jesus some more when you're ready."

"Sure. Your story?"

Chester's eyes glistened. One lone tear dropped from his right eye. He let it. "My daughter was kidnapped when she was fifteen. A beautiful girl. Much like you. Mature for her age. And some guy grabbed her and sold her into slavery."

"Slavery? You mean like picking cotton or something?"

Chester shook his head. "You've been a slave as well. Sexual slave. Serving men sexually for someone else. That's what they forced Brittany to do." Tears streamed from his eyes.

"I guess I never thought of it that way. Figured I deserved it."

Chester grabbed Sara's hand and held it in both of his. "No one deserves that. No one. You are God's creation, and you deserve to be treated like His creation."

Sara slowly slipped her hand out. "Who'd you kill?"

"The man who kidnapped Brittany."

"Did you find her?"

He nodded. "But like Carolyn, Brittany overdosed before I got to her."

"So, that's why you help Mr. Rockport?" she asked quickly because she felt more tears coming. What was going on with her?

Chester nodded. "And because Mr. Rockport got me out of prison after serving three of my twenty-year sentence."

Sara lost her battle and dissolved into tears. She put her head in her hands and cried harder than she ever had in her entire life. Her body shuddered. She felt a hand on her back, then felt herself pulled into a hug. The door opened. Footsteps approached. Another set of arms wrapped around her. She looked up enough to see Dr. Cortez. She glanced at the door. Mr. Rockport stood in the doorway, tears pouring out of his eyes as well. Great. She'd started a cryfest. Hopefully, no one she knew would ever hear about this. Sara Hanley didn't cry. But she was and it felt wonderful.

Sara loaded the last of that night's dinner dishes into the dishwasher. It had been her second attempt at cooking for the two men, Rockport and Chester. Homemade spaghetti sauce, a recipe she'd found online. It turned out edible, unlike the first time, when she'd tried making tuna casserole and burnt it to a crisp.

Rockport and Chester left shortly after dinner, back to the streets to look for someone who needed rescuing. Being alone in the house creeped Sara out. Visions of Keyshawn Williams or Big Eddie's goons crashing in and snatching her looped in her head. So quiet. They needed a dog or something. Rockport had nixed that idea, not knowing if future guests would be allergic.

She wandered into the family room and plopped down on the off-white sofa. So much white. Not as much as Big Eddie's place, but still she never felt like she could eat snacks while watching television, afraid she'd spot the furniture. She snatched the remote and flipped on the large-screen television mounted over the gray-stone fireplace. She wasn't sure how to start a fire. While watching some stupid police show, she kept glancing at the glass doors on both sides of the room. She wished Rockport would put curtains on them so no one could see in. Shadows played over both sets of glass from the wind blowing the trees in the backyard that ran alongside the pool. Moonlight shimmered on the water's surface and caused weird lighting on the windows. Each time something moved, she thought someone was there.

Behind her, the front door burst open. She launched off the couch, ready to run. But Rockport walked through carrying someone's legs. A woman. Chester followed, holding the woman's upper body. Sara walked over to them.

The young woman, probably early twenties, seemed unconscious. Chester and Rockport carried her into the living room and laid her on the sofa.

"Who's this?" Sara asked. "You kidnap her too?"

"Not sure her name," Chester answered. "Found her in an alley. Some guy dumped her there. She must have passed out on him."

"She a prostitute?"

Chester gave her a sarcastic look.

The woman wore a short skirt, black fishnet stockings, heels, and a low-cut midriff blouse. "Okay, yeah, she's a street girl. Who's her pimp?"

"Don't know. Didn't see anyone."

Sara bent over and examined her. Short black hair curled under her chin, and she had a round face with hollowed out cheeks. "She still alive?"

The woman moaned and shifted.

"Guess so." Sara stepped back. "What are we going to do with her?"

"We?" Rockport asked.

"Yeah, we." Sara gestured to indicate the three of them.

Rockport stepped over to Sara and hugged her. "I'm so glad to hear you say that."

Sara pulled out of the embrace and looked at Rockport. "You're a strange old man."

Rockport chuckled. "I'll go call Dr. Cortez. Remember her, Sara?"

Sara nodded.

"You and Chester stay with her." Rockport hurried out of the living room.

Sara perched on the edge of the sofa near the woman's shoulders and watched her breathe erratically. "She OD'd on something." She looked at the woman's arms. No needle marks. She took the woman's shoes off. The stockings had holes in them anyway, so she ripped them to examine her feet. Nothing between the toes. "Probably not meth or heroin."

Chester hovered over them, his massive arms crossed.

Thirty minutes later, Dr. Cortez arrived. The woman had not yet awakened. Dr. Cortez convinced Rockport that the woman needed to be taken to the hospital. Rockport and Chester carried her back out to the car. Sara watched them drive off to Mercy Hospital. Dr. Cortez followed them in her Audi.

After they left, Sara backed up to the door, scanning the neighborhood, hoping none of Big Eddie's goons were hiding behind trees waiting for their chance to grab her. She felt the doorknob behind her, jumped inside, slammed the door, and locked it.

*****

Sara fell asleep waiting for the two men. When she woke up, sunlight filled the family room through the east facing glass door. She padded upstairs, showered, and dressed in fresh clothes. Rockport continually bought her new outfits. She had moved into one of the guest rooms. Unfortunately, she was taller and thicker than Rockport's daughter had been, so the closets already full of clothing didn't fit her.

She went downstairs to the kitchen and ate some Grape Nuts. After eating, she put her bowl in the dishwasher and started toward the family room for more mind-numbing television. A key turning in the front door stopped her before she could sit down. She reversed direction and waited.

Rockport and Chester entered. Between them, the woman from the night before shuffled, using the two men as support. She offered a slight smile to Sara. The men led the woman into the living room and let her sit on the same sofa she'd been laid on the night before. Sara joined them. She sat in a zebra patterned armchair and stared at the woman.

The woman stared back.

Rockport tapped Sara on the shoulder. "Why don't you introduce yourself?"

"Oh, yeah, sorry. Hi, I'm Sara. These guys kidnapped me off the street and now I live here."

Chester laughed.

The woman looked up at him. "That true?" Her voice came out scratchy and deep.

67

"Yea, that's pretty much true."

The woman looked at Sara. "Were you a street walker?"

"At the end of the life, yes. Not how I started, though."

"Oh. I'm Marsha. Nice to meet you, Sara."

Sara smiled. "What did you OD on?"

Marsha's eyes widened. She didn't answer right away.

Rockport sat in the other zebra-patterned armchair. "You'll have to excuse Sara. She can be a bit direct."

"What did I say?" Sara asked.

"It's okay. Painkillers. Oxy."

"Ha." Sara looked at Rockport. "I told you it wasn't meth or heroin."

"Yes, you did. Ms. Marsha here is, or was, a nurse. And we didn't kidnap her. She's here voluntarily. Dr. Cortez has agreed to help her detox from the painkillers. And Marsha has agreed to stay on as our resident nurse."

"Why? Are you or Chester sick? I'm not sick, anymore."

"Not for us, Sara. For the girls we will be bringing here."

"You're going to kidnap more girls?"

"Kidnap is a strong word. We're intervening. Helping them. Like we did you."

"Yeah, but you kidnapped me."

Marsha shifted in the sofa. "Can I get some water?"

Chester left for the kitchen.

"Sara, did they help you, though?" Marsha asked.

"Yes, they did. I'm not hooking anymore. Not doing heroin no more. And I'm learning to use the computer. That's pretty cool. Mr. Rockport said I could be his administrative assistant once I'm prof, profi. What was that word?"

"Proficient, dear."

"Yeah, that."

Chester returned and handed Marsha a glass of water.

"If you were a nurse," Sara said, "why did you start hooking?"

A shadow passed behind Marsha's eyes. She took a large drink of water then placed the glass on a table close to her. Before answering, she studied her hands. Chipped nails with fading polish. Sara'd been there done that.

"I injured myself in a hospital basketball league. Pain isn't my thing. My doctor put me on oxy. I took more than I should and got hooked. I started seeing two other doctors, unknown to each other, so I could get more. Oxy isn't cheap." She took another drink of water and looked past all of them. "I showed up to work high one day and made a bad mistake. A patient nearly died because of me. The hospital fired me." Tears formed in her eyes. A few drops rolled down her cheeks.

Sara said, "It's okay. I get it. You don't have to tell me more."

"No, I do. I need to say it out loud. I spent all my money on painkillers. I lost my house, my car. With no food, I had to do something. The first time after I sold myself, I puked my guts out."

Sara muttered, "At least you had a choice." She expected Marsha to get angry at her but didn't care. The woman's sob story irritated her.

Instead, Marsha said, "I'm so sorry you didn't have that choice."

That floored Sara. "I didn't mean anything by that."

"It's okay. They told me your story in the car over here. At least what you've told them. And I can imagine there is much more. I'm telling you my story not because I think I've had it rougher than you. I'm telling you so we can be open with each other. I'm hoping you can help me, and I can help you get past all this junk."

Tears burned Sara's eyes. Not again. Sara Hanley didn't cry. She wasn't about to cry in front of this woman. She wiped her eyes with the back of her hand.

"Anyway, after that, it was easier, especially when I had enough oxy. The other night I took too much before my next customer. I guess I passed out on him. And I guess, from what the guys said, he dumped me in an alley."

"Yeah, that's what they said. They found you in an alley."

Marsha gazed away again. Her chest moved in and out with heavy breaths. "I thank God they found me and brought me here. And I pray that God will heal me." She looked at Sara with an intense gaze. "And I pray God will heal you, as well."

"Yeah, thanks. Chester has been telling me about God quite a bit."

"And I'll keep telling you until you confess Jesus as Lord."

"Whatever."

Rockport said, "Why don't you take Marsha upstairs and show her one of the empty guest rooms."

Sara did. And they talked in that room for three hours. She'd never told so much of her life story to anyone before. And when she went to bed, for the first time she could remember, the incredible weight that had always pushed her down and kept her down lightened. Not gone, but less. She wondered what it would take to rid herself completely of that burden. The weird visions she'd had of that priest, the ghost church, Jesus, and even the moving statue played through her mind. She decided God had been watching over her and maybe tomorrow she needed one more conversation with Chester.

The young girl named Ashley stared wide-eyed, partially opened mouth. When Sara stopped talking about her life, Ashley looked down. Her hands did acrobatics in her lap. When she looked up, tears reflected in her eyes.

"I ran away. I . . . I had this boyfriend. At least I thought he was a boyfriend. Kind of like your boyfriend, Jesse."

Sara tsked. "Yeah, some boyfriend, huh? Did your *boyfriend* do the same to you?"

Ashley nodded. "He was older, too. He told me he was sixteen, but now, I don't know. He might have been even older."

Sara leaned in and rubbed Ashley's shoulder. "You thought you found someone who understood you, right? Someone who said they loved you?"

Again, Ashley nodded. "At first, he treated me so well. At least he never, you know, made me have sex with anyone."

"Then what?"

"He convinced me to run away." She looked up at the ceiling. "My parents are probably frantic, wondering where I am."

Sara narrowed her eyes, then grabbed Ashley's hand. "Your parents? Is your home a safe place?"

"Oh yeah. They love me, I'm sure."

"Then why did you run away?" She wished she'd had a home to return to.

"My dad, he's a preacher, a minister. He had a lot of rules for me, you know?"

Being constrained by rules, Sara couldn't relate to that. Her foster parents had made rules, but she'd followed very few of them. She shrugged, hoping Ashley would continue. Someone came down the basement stairs. Probably Marsha to check on the girl.

"Go ahead," Sara prompted.

"Robert, my boyfriend, convinced me to go with him. And I did. We lived together for a while. He had an apartment. Said his parents kicked him out. Told me his dad was a minister too, and he hated all the rules."

"Probably all a lie."

Ashley's eyes widened.

Oops. Sara decided she needed to keep commentary to herself. "Sorry. Go on."

"Anyway, after a couple months he brought me to this big dude who had a great house outside Forest Park."

"Big Eddie?"

"Yeah, that's the guy. He was so nice to me. Let me stay at his house a couple days. But one day they gave me something to try. I smoked it, thinking it was pot, but it smelled funny."

"Meth."

"Yeah, I guess. But I got hooked. Then Big Eddie gave me to Keyshawn. The same one you worked for, right?"

"Yup."

"And the days and nights started blending together. I'd hit the meth between customers, so I wouldn't feel anything. Then that big guy upstairs carried me out of the strip joint. And I came here."

The door opened. Marsha walked in with a tray. Sandwich, apple, and water. "Lunch is served." She smiled and placed the tray on the one other piece of furniture in the bleak plywood room, a nightstand with a single drawer and shelf below.

Sara stood. "Thanks for listening to me, Ashley."

Ashley smiled at her. "Thank you for telling me your story and why you're still here." She grabbed the sandwich but hesitated. "Maybe I should stay as well. But you know what I really want to do?"

"What?" Sara asked.

"Go home. To my parents."

Sara and Marsha looked at each other. Grins broke out on their faces.

Sara said, "I think that can be arranged. Let me talk to Mr. Rockport."

*****

Sara felt the weight of Mandy's stare. The young blonde girl waited. Expected. Anticipated. This girl was so much like Sara herself. Tall, blonde, tough, and sixteen-years-old. Chester and Rockport had grabbed her out of a motel room two months ago, but she still occupied one of the two plywood rooms in the basement. She still insisted on being set free, though she had nowhere to go other than back to the street or back to Slice, her pimp, to work the cheap motels.

Today, though, Mandy was subdued. Sara had confronted her. Yelled at her.

"You know my story. And you're not that much different. You want to leave? You want to go back to shooting up and having sex with greasy strangers? Fine with me. See if I care."

Expecting a tirade from Mandy mirroring previous shouting matches they'd had, Sara was floored when the girl sheepishly said, "I thought you did care. I . . . I thought you were my friend."

Sara melted. She sat on the bed and hugged Mandy. "I am, hun. Sorry. But you need to stay here longer, until we can figure out where you can safely go."

They remained embraced for a few minutes. Mandy pushed back.

"Didn't you tell me Jesus was one reason you stayed here?"

"Yes. Jesus gives me the strength to resist going back to the life. To stay and help others like you."

"Tell me who Jesus is? How can He help me?"

Eels swam in Sara's belly. She felt comfortable with her own faith. She'd said things here and there, given Jesus credit for her emotional health. but she'd never had to present the Gospel to anyone else. What if she messed it up? What if, because of what she said, this young girl would never accept Christ? She remembered something Chester had told her. When in doubt, pray. And that's what she did. Silently, she asked Jesus to help her tell Mandy about Him. She asked God to give her the words to say.

And He did.

After explaining to Mandy that Jesus was born of a virgin, lived a perfect life, and sacrificed Himself on the cross for everyone, then rose again from the dead, she asked, "Do you want to pray to give your life to Jesus?"

Tears filled Mandy's eyes. "I still don't see how anyone can love me. Why would God or Jesus want me?"

Oh boy. Now she had to answer a deep theological question. She lifted up more prayers, asking for wisdom on what to say. Another story Chester had shared way back when she'd first arrived came to her mind, about a courtroom and someone offering to pay for a crime for someone else. She told Mandy the same story.

"See, God is that judge, but because of what Jesus did, God only sees Jesus. He doesn't see what we did. As long as we believe in Jesus and surrender our lives to Him."

Mandy stared at her. Sara wasn't answering her question, she could sense that. Another thought came to her. Paul.

"There was this dude, the one who wrote many of the books in the New Testament—the newer part of the Bible. His name was Paul."

"Uh huh. Chester's told me about him."

"Yeah, well he was a killer. Did you know that?"

Mandy's eyes grew large. She shook her round head. "Who'd he kill?"

"Christians. Until Jesus asked him why he was doing that and then told Paul to go to some town to meet some other dude. But anyway, Paul became one of God's most faithful preachers. If God can love a murderer, He can certainly love us."

"I suppose. What do I need to do?"

Sara led Mandy in the prayer to confess Jesus as Lord and give her life to Him. After she finished, Mandy threw her arms around her and cried. They stayed like that for several minutes.

Mandy pushed away. "Thank you so much for telling me that. And . . . and for being my friend."

The door opened. Marsha came in with lunch. Sara hugged Mandy again, then left to allow Mandy to eat her lunch. Marsha met her upstairs.

"How'd it go?"

Sara stammered, sputtered, coughed. Every time she started to say what had just happened, she choked up.

Marsha gave her a side hug. "Something amazing, seems like."

Sara nodded, then managed to say, "Mandy accepted Jesus. And I led her in the prayer. Me! I can't believe it."

"You and God, girl. You and God can do anything." Marsha gave her a full hug. "Go tell Mr. Rockport. He'll be so excited."

Sara raced up to the second floor and banged on Rockport's office door.

"Come in."

Sara opened the door and walked in. Rockport sat behind his massive, antique wooden desk in a huge leather executive chair with a cell phone to his ear. He held up a finger to her, indicating to wait a bit.

She stood in front of the desk, clasping her hands together in front of her and moving from foot to foot. When she started to hum, Rockport shot her an annoyed look. She stopped and instead paced the office. Her face began to hurt, but she couldn't remove the smile.

Rockport said goodbye to whomever he was speaking with and put the cell phone down. "Looks like you're a bit excited. Did something happen?"

She rushed to his desk, slammed her hands on it, and leaned over close to him. "Mandy. I . . . she . . . I can't believe it. I led her to Christ. Me! I did that. Well, God did it through me."

Rockport stood. A smile bloomed on his face. They hugged over the desk. "That's wonderful, Sara. See, I knew you could connect to these girls and help them."

Sara pulled away. "I think she's ready."

"Ready? For what?"

"To be let out of that awful room. To be given the freedom of the house."

Rockport's smile faded. He touched his chin and scrunched his brows. "Wasn't it just yesterday that she argued with you about leaving again?"

"But that was before. Now she has Jesus, and she said she wants to stay until we find a safe place for her."

"And she can't go home?"

"There is no home for her to go to. And she's sixteen. No one will want to foster her, especially given her background. Besides, I'd never condemn someone to foster care."

"Not all foster care parents are bad, Sara. Most are good people trying to help kids in bad situations. I know you had some poor experiences." He sighed and sat. "Let me poke around and see if I can find a family that might take her in."

"Okay. In the meantime, can we let her out of that box?"

He nodded. "But talk to Chester and Marsha and let them know before you do."

"Deal." Sara ran out of the office and down to the first floor, then down to the basement. She knocked on Mandy's door.

"Come in."

Sara walked in. "Guess what?"

All the food on Mandy's tray was gone. A good sign. "What?"

"I'm getting you out of this room. Hold tight. I'll be right back."

Mandy smiled, then jumped up and ran to Sara. They hugged, then Sara left to go tell Chester and Marsha.

Eight days later, after Mandy had been missing for three days, Rockport and Chester returned to the house after searching for her. Sara waited for them right inside the front door.

"I'm waiting for a call." Rockport breezed by her. "Check with me in an hour." He headed upstairs.

An hour later, to the second, Sara walked upstairs. Each step felt heavier than the last. Did they find her? Who was he waiting for? At his office door, she knocked.

"Come in, Sara."

She sucked in a deep breath, opened the door, and walked into the plush office. Normally, she'd sit in one of the armchairs fronting the massive desk. But she could tell the news wasn't good by the fallen look on Rockport's face.

Rockport pocketed his iPhone, stood, and came around his desk. He took both Sara's hands in his like they were about to dance. "That was Detective Warren. They found Mandy." He swallowed hard.

Sara started to tremble. Her lips quivered. She prepared to scream.

"I'm sorry, Sara. She's dead."

No scream, just a low moan. "Nooo." She collapsed against Rockport.

He hugged her tight and whispered, "It was an overdose."

"No." Anger broadsided her. She pushed away from Rockport. "No! She wouldn't have done that. She was . . . she was done. Over with it. I know she was."

"It's possible she didn't inject herself. But the cops didn't find any evidence suggesting someone forced it on her."

"They must have. Her pimp. She wouldn't have gotten high on her own."

"She was an addict, Sara. It's always a possibility."

"No. She was done. I know she was."

The anger dissipated. She collapsed into the armchair and stared straight ahead, seeing nothing but Mandy's long, blonde hair, her bright-blue eyes, and her huge smile eight days ago when Sara had told her she had free rein of the house.

"She was ready. I was so sure of it. I was so sure of it."

Chapter 14

The memory of Mandy haunted Sara as she descended the stairs to talk with Angel, the latest girl Rockport and Chester had kidnapped. She never ceased to remind them they were kidnapping these girls. Lovingly reminded them, of course.

For the last seven months, since Mandy's death, Sara had become Rockport's administrative assistant. She helped Marsha when needed with new girls. Angel was the first they'd grabbed in a while. The house was filling up. But most of the girls there now had been like Marsha, dragged in off the street in bad shape. A couple had even come on their own when asked, wanting to give up the life, but not sure how. Rockport's house was huge, but still, things were getting crowded.

She stood outside the locked room in the basement. The other two rooms were empty, doors open. Inside the locked room they'd put Angel, whom Rockport had brought in much the same way he'd brought Sara herself under the guise of being a customer. He'd drugged her as well, and the girl was not happy when she woke up. Déjà vu all over again, as someone famous once said. Some baseball dude or someone.

She knocked softly.[1]

"It's your house, come on in," Angel said.

"Are you going to behave?" Sara asked.

"Are you going to stick me with anything?"

"I haven't stuck you yet."

"Don't be funny. You know what I mean."

"It's just me. No needles."

"Then I suppose I'll behave. I'm sure Godzilla is with you anyway."

Sara opened the door, slipped in, and closed the door behind her. "Actually, it's just me. And if you've forgotten, I'm Sara."

---

[1] This section to the end is from *An Angel and a One-Armed Man* by B.D. Lawrence. The first book in the One-Armed Man series.

Angel was sitting on the bed, leaning against the wall, feet out straight. Sara sat at the foot of the bed.

"How are you feeling?"

"Crappy."

"It'll be that way for a few days."

Angel said nothing for a minute, just stared at Sara. She narrowed her eyes and scrunched her brows. "How long you keeping me here?"

"That depends."

"On what? And why are you keeping me here?"

Sara moved further up the bed and smiled at Angel. "Please believe me, we're here to help you."

"Yeah, right. By locking me up and sticking me with needles full of God knows what." Her eyes blazed. She squeezed her fists closed, taking a handful of sheet in each.

"Not only does God know, but I know, and I'll tell you." Sara smiled. Angel continued to frown. "The pill you didn't take is Suboxone. The shot was Methadone. I'd really prefer you take the pill. Less side effects and not addictive. Both are to help you through your withdrawal."

"I don't want help through withdrawal. I want a fix."

"And that's why you're locked up."

Angel crossed her arms and brought her knees up to her chin. Her demeanor deflated. She no longer looked like the streetwise hooker she thought she was, but a lost little child.

"I just want to go home."

"Really? Is that really where you want to go?"

Angel slowly shook her head. "No, I can't go there."

"Why not?"

"I just can't." She dipped her head and squeezed herself into an even tighter ball. Sara reached out and stroked her hair.

"Right now, this is the safest place for you."

Angel looked up, her eyes glistening. "And where is here? Where am I?"

"You're in a big house in Huntleigh Woods."

"I . . . I don't know where that is. I've only been here a few months. This still St. Louis?"

"Yup. Real nice neighborhood."

Angel put her head down again and rocked slightly back and forth.

Sara resumed stroking her hair. "If it means anything, I know exactly what you're going through."

"Yeah, right. Did you have to run away from home then have sex with sweaty, disgusting men for money?"

"Yup."

Angel looked up, her eyes wide. "Really?"

"I was a hooker just like you."

"You from some little cow town, too? Coming here to the big city to get away from a bad scene? Thinking it can't be that hard to live on your own?"

Sara hesitated, deciding if she wanted this conversation to go where it was going. But Rockport had told her if she wanted to get close to someone, she had to make herself vulnerable, she had to open herself up. But the last time she'd done that with Mandy, the girl had OD'd. Did she want to take that chance again? She sucked in a deep breath. What the heck, she thought. Why not?

Author's Note

If you're interested in following more of Sara Hanley's life, please check out the <u>One-Armed Detective series</u>.

Thank you for reading *Sara's Story*. She had a brutal life, yet was rescued by Calvin Rockport and Chester Henderson, then redeemed by Jesus Christ. I pray her life is a hyperbole, that there are no girls going through everything she went through. However, there are thousands of girls living through many of the situations that Sara went through.

The intent of this story is to give you a view of what sex-trafficking looks like in our country. It's not even close to all-inclusive. One estimate I read said that there are more than 60,000 points of prostitution (where sex can be bought) in the United States; more locations than Starbucks has. Sara's Story shows just a few of those. Massage parlors, strip clubs, the street, and houses.

Jesse, her supposed boyfriend, represents victims being trafficked by family members or close friends. Over half of all victims are trafficked by family or close friends. Through Jesse we also see the manipulation that takes place for at-risk girls. Having been abandoned by her mother and moved from foster home to foster home, Sara is desperately seeking love and attention. These are the type of at-risk girls that predators like Jesse target.

Being private citizens rescuing trafficked girls, Calvin Rockport and Chester Henderson, are an anomaly. This is where literary license comes in. But there are many organizations that do rescue and rehabilitate sex-trafficked victims. And you have an opportunity to help fight this evil scourge.

I give half of my proceeds from every book I sell to an organization in Phoenix that rescues and rehabilitates sex-trafficked girls.

Thank you again for reading *Sara's Story*. And please check out the <u>One-Armed Detective series</u> available in eBook and paperback on Amazon.

B.D. Lawrence.

Streams of the Heart

by Shannon McNear

84

For those who feel unseen and unknown . . . your Maker sees, and knows.

Chapter One

Sacagawea

Where does a story begin?

Is it with the moment of one's birth? Of awakening awareness to the world around them? Or only when one first begins a task which will change not only her life but that of those around her?

I cannot say when I was born, although my mother told me I made my appearance during a star-filled, moonlit night in full summer. The story of my people in the time before flowed through and around me as I grew like a snow-fed river through the woven basket of a fishing weir.

I recall a lush river valley rimmed with hills. Summers of blinding brilliance and vivid beauty. Night skies glittering so brightly with stars they appeared like the sun glinting off a frosty meadow. The dread and wonder of the northern lights, like the dance of our ancestors high above us. The bitter cold and howling winds of winter, where we kept snug inside our homes and shared well-known songs and tales.

My mother—and the rest of my family—taught me the joy of work, the satisfaction of a task well done. Whether it was in catching and preparing the *agai* during their early summer run up the rivers, or traveling far with our people the *Agai 'dika* to hunt the buffalo, I sought only to do well, to serve well, no matter where I found myself.

I never knew heartbreak, until the day *they* came.

The sun beat down upon us without mercy. My captors showed no sign of being bothered by it, mounted as they were, but my feet and head ached from the endless walking. I sneaked glances at their cruel faces, darker than those of my people, their black hair braided smoothly on either side of their heads, bows, tomahawks, and other weapons strapped to their bodies. The Minnetaree came from across the plains, slaying many of my people while taking others captive.

Captives that included me.

I thought of my mother as she went down beneath a Minnetaree hatchet while I hid in the willows beside the river. It felt like the weapon was embedded in my own heart.

My mother and aunties always warned us of the possibility that such a thing could happen and instructed us that if we were taken, we should do our best to submit and survive.

I did not know why I had been spared, or how I would continue to draw breath. Yet somehow I did, despite witnessing my mother's death, the endless walking, and the tears that welled up when I least wanted them. Arriving at the Minnetaree town brought little relief. The women scolded and the children laughed, but we could hardly understand a word. The other girls and I whispered to each other whenever we could. My closest friend told me she planned to escape and that I should do the same. When at last she found opportunity to do so, she managed to slip away while I was caught and brought back.

My spirit finally broke at that. I gave myself to laboring as hard for the people who took me as I would have for those of my birth—indeed, more. I gave respect even to those to whom it was not due. I applied myself to learning their tongue and their ways. I came of age as a woman and became aware of the assessing looks from the men. Then one day, I was told I would be given not to a warrior of the Minnetaree, but to one of the ugly, bearded trappers from the north, who had won me in a game of chance.

Even then, I did not protest. I did not resist. I let them give me to this man, even when I learned I would not be the only one, that he had taken another to wife before me.

But it would lessen the burden of our work as women for there to be two of us. And as Otter Woman also was Agai'dika, we could share talk in the speech of our birth. This and more I told myself, for it would do no good to resist or even protest the situation. I would, instead, make the best of it.

Then came the day Husband had a great announcement.

He sat a little straighter by the fire and fixed both Otter Woman and me with a proud look. "I have been hired by the white men journeying toward the setting sun to help speak with your people on the way." He fell silent, sucking his teeth. "One of you will go with me to also help with that."

Otter Woman drew herself up a little. I turned back to my task of stitching the covering of what was to be a swaddle or the lining of a cradleboard. Even now, the child danced within me. Of course I would not be chosen. And what would become of me and my little one with the man who called himself husband gone from here?

"Otter Woman," he said, "you have been a good wife. But you have been away from your people for more years than Bird Woman, and so her remembrance of your shared tongue will certainly be greater."

"What are you saying, Husband?" Otter Woman asked.

"I am saying that I will be taking Bird Woman and the child when the white hunters continue on their journey."

Otter Woman surged to her feet. I simply could not move.

Had I heard him aright? I would be going along?

Thoughts burst within me, like sparks when a carefully laid fire collapses upon the embers. The baby—all I would need for its care. The company of white men who I did not know. The privations of travel. Seeing again the mountains I had loved so much as a child. And . . . my people, though the likelihood of truly seeing them again was very low.

"She? She is to go, and not me?" Otter Woman's voice shrilled to the top of our lodge.

Our husband gave a single nod. "Even so."

I kept my head down and continued stitching.

"You have no answer to this, Bird Woman?"

I looked up, gauging Otter Woman's response. She still stood, this time glaring at me. "I will do whatever you decide is best," I said, keeping my own voice level.

And so we moved our lodge into the enclosed area the white men were building, where lodges smaller than ours would serve as dwelling places for the winter. Husband told us they were unaccustomed to the cold. Otter Woman and I smiled a little. We could understand that.

The white men were led by two who I learned to recognize except when they were bundled thoroughly against the cold. One seemed more lively, with brownish hair and eyes the color of sky—whether they were of a clouded sky or clear, I could not tell—while the other, more somber, had hair the color of fire and darker eyes. Cap-ten Loo-ess the first was called. Cap-ten Klark was the other.

Both eyed Otter Woman and I with interest and curiosity at gatherings, but only spoke with our husband. Not that we expected anything else.

*****

Clark—December 1804

I never knew winter could be so bitter.

Were it not for the friendly folk of the upper Missouri, I am certain we would have perished. The river was near to freezing for the season, we were informed, and so we determined to settle in until such time as we could once more navigate those waters.

But, oh the cold. And I, who am not unacquainted with hardship, found it more harsh than I ever dreamed possible.

We all did. And it was by mutual agreement that we determined none could blame us for taking warmth where it was offered.

At first, however, some of us earnestly sought to honor the rules of propriety. I was ever mindful of Julia, who I hoped someday to wed but yet remained in Virginia, so sweet and young and innocent. I would not forbid others their enjoyment of Indian hospitality (for so it was, as they fair persecuted us with their favors at times), but I determined to resist.

In the meantime, we built a fort and small houses, which we called Fort Mandan after one of the local peoples, and settled in for the winter to prepare for the rest of our journey. We made inquiries of the Indians on the rivers to the west, where they might lead, and whether there might be a waterway to take us all the way to the Pacific Ocean.

The greater part of our labor, as it had been from the Illinois and up the river, was to persuade the Indian peoples of the preference and necessity of peace with each other and with the United States government. We made speeches and gave gifts, mostly small things like medals, handkerchiefs, and strings of beads, but they often seemed well pleased with these. And most agreed—at least in spirit—with the idea of living in peace but would often give testimony to how this neighboring people or that had made war on them.

They could be very tiresome, but to this end were all our energies focused, in addition to laying by the necessities of life during this long, cold, bitter season.

We had started the journey with a company of men handpicked for their bravery, hunting ability, and survival knowledge. Several engagés, or contract boatmen, were added to the party near St. Louis, where the journey began. Later, we hired a handful of Frenchmen who knew the tongue of the Indians to help us communicate with the peoples we encountered on our way up the Missouri River. It was a matter of policy to choose unmarried men, so none of us were initially inclined to accept the services of Toussaint Charbonneau, a French trapper of no particular merit who dwelt near our Fort with his two wives. The man spoke only French and Hidatsa, but we learned that his wives were of a people we called the Snake, or at least that was the translation given of the Indian hand sign for their name. These people lived at the edge of the great mountains and were sure to know the best way to cross, so we thought it possibly prudent to take him and one of his women along to help translate and negotiate for horses.

To make matters worse, however, we learned that the wife he thought best to take was expecting a baby. Not only must we wait for the river to thaw and be navigable again, but we would have the needs of a woman and child to consider.

Providence have mercy upon us.

Chapter Two

Sacagawea

"Why are they here?" Otter Woman muttered. "Men have no place at the birth of a child, much less these filthy white men."

I gulped for air, the pang easing but little before wrapping my body in its embrace once more. I could spare no strength for a reply as a moan broke from my throat.

One man in particular watched me, his hair a dull brown in the dimness of our lodge, eyes crinkling in what appeared concern. I knew he was considered skilled in the healing arts.

None of that mattered in the moment, as my pangs swept me away.

The child moved inside me, as if protesting the process. Between pangs, I cradled my belly and murmured to him before my breath was again taken away. My groan became a wail, and I swayed on my feet.

Across the lodge, the men watched and muttered to each other. Otter Woman threw more sage into the fire. After a brief, earnest conversation, the brown-haired man ducked outside.

The wind howled against the walls of the lodge. A matching howl rose from inside me as the storm within my own body raged.

After a time, which could have been a few moments or half a day, the man returned, handing something to the trader Jessaume who also worked with the white men. Jessaume crumbled it into a cup, and they spoke with Otter Woman, gesturing between the cup and me. She hesitated at first, then came to me. "He bids you drink. It is the crushed rattle from a snake. It may help the babe come more easily."

I held no confidence in the substance to do what he claimed, but stranger things had taken place, and medicine could be surprising. I choked down the contents of the cup, swallowing the gritty flakes on my tongue, then immediately returned to the half crouch I had adopted to accommodate the crushing pressure inside me.

Otter Woman lost patience with the watching men and shooed them out of the lodge.

While she scolded, the pressure moved downward, and before I knew it, the babe had made his way into the world through me.

Otter Woman handed me my child, slippery and wet and bleating, and hastened to tuck me into my pallet. I caught a glimpse of the trader Jessaume still lingering at the lodge opening, his dark eyes wide. I could laugh at his wonder, but a rush of something I had not felt since being held in my own mother's arms filled me, and I had no attention to spare for the oddity of men in my lodge.

The tiny thing in my arms had quieted and now regarded me as steadily as I did him. "Welcome to the world, little man," I murmured, stroking his soft cheek.

The means by which he came to me may not have been entirely of my own will, but I would not refuse the gift of his life. Who knows how Creator may use him in his lifetime? Or me either, for that matter?

I thought of the journey to come, where Husband and I would accompany the strange white men on their journey toward the setting sun, in search of passage across the great mountains.

Perhaps that was why the white healer had felt compelled to aid me in this little one's birth.

*****

Clark—February 11, 1805

Silence. Blessed silence.

We had marked the hours, then minutes, by the thin wail issuing from one of the two Indian lodges that stood in the fort yard, rising above the wind and the other sounds of camp, lifting the small hairs on the back of my neck. For a long while, Captain Lewis peered out the door in the direction of its source, then glanced at his timepiece while he raked a hand through his untidy hair.

An entire day had the younger Indian wife of Charbonneau labored, and we were no more accustomed to the sounds of her cries than when it had first started. The wails now alternated every minute, according to my own timepiece.

"It is her first," he mused, "so the tediousness is perhaps not to be wondered at."

Was he trying to reassure himself as well as me? I gave a noncommittal sound, but a tightness still gathered my brows and shoulders. The thought tugged at me of that doe-eyed young woman, so calm and sweet, in any sort of distress.

The fact that she was bound to that skunk of a man, Toussant Charbonneau, was a doubly bitter draught to swallow, but I tucked that observation aside. The French trader might yet prove his worth.

Furthermore, this child's safe arrival was but one step on the next stage of our journey. We must not only wait for the woman to regain her strength, but for the ice to fully break before setting out again upriver. Though the cold was slightly less bitter than it had been, it was nothing like comfortable enough for travel yet.

At last Lewis sighed and cast me a glance. "I will go over to see if I might help in any way."

"Not likely," I quipped, more lightly than I felt. He gave me a nod before stepping out into the wind.

In short order he returned, only to rummage in the stacks of baggage taking up one wall of our hut. "Rattlesnake tail," he tossed over his shoulder while he searched. "Jessaume insists he has used it to good effect and that it never fails to bring forth the babe speedily."

"Rattlesnake tail."

Lewis straightened with a small bundle in his hand. "We will see, I suppose." He laughed drily, shaking his head and disappearing out the door. I stepped to where I could watch him running across the space toward the Indian lodge.

Another minute or two marked by the Indian woman's wails, then Lewis, Jessaume, and another pair of men emerged from the lodge. Lewis made his way back across the yard but Jessaume lingered at the lodge opening.

Lewis returned to watching at the door of our hut, seemingly unaffected by the cold.

The wails changed in pitch, then fell away completely. The silence rang as all within the fort stopped, waiting.

The trader popped back into view and called out, "She is delivered of a fine boy!"

The entire fort burst into cheering.

Chapter Three

Sacagawea

Husband gave the babe a name in his own speech, but I just called him "Little One." As the weather warmed enough for the river to flow, I grew less fatigued from the birth, and Little One also grew. My preparations for the journey were as complete as I could make them. I had built his cradleboard with care, as the women of the village had taught me, and gathered all I would need for tending to him.

One calm day, as I walked outside to test the cradleboard, the fire-haired leader approached, gesturing toward the burden I carried. I turned so he could see Little One's face, and his own bloomed with a rare grin. "Bébé?" I asked, in the speech of my husband, and he laughed.

"Bébé," he agreed, and though I did not understand the rest of his words, his tone was kindly.

We women had heard all manner of talk about these men. The ones who were eager to take advantage of the women's favors and the ones who were reluctant. Most curious of all was the tall man with skin so dark he seemed crafted of the night itself, who appeared to be a servant of the fire-haired leader but sported freely with our people. He was strong and seemed honorable enough.

At last, the day arrived for our departure. The men set me in one of their great canoes where many provisions were piled up, and before long, they pushed off from the shore.

The motion and lap of the water entranced me immediately. I had forgotten how blue was the sky, how open the plains, but I renewed my acquaintance with both as we traveled upstream—sometimes pushed by poles, sometimes rowed, and sometimes drawn by something they called a *sail*.

I might, Creator willing, see the furthest edge of these lands. Might even see my own people again, on the way.

But that was too much to hope for, so I refused to let myself dwell upon it.

The early days were full of wonder for me, the delight of open skies and new sights. The excitement of the men who had hired us was a contagious thing, and their laughter and calls to each other echoed from boat to boat. *Pirogue,* Husband called the two largest boats.

I felt snug in my place, sheltered enough to nurse Little One as needed. The men eyed me and asked, through my husband, whether I was comfortable enough thus, but I assured him all was well.

I missed Otter Woman and the other girls of the Agai'dika. Husband and a couple of the others could speak Hidatsa, the speech of those who had stolen me from my own people, but otherwise there was no one I could understand directly. An unexpected comfort was when the great furry dog owned by one of the leaders came to sit beside me and Little One in the boat. He sniffed at us, and I scratched under his ears. His tongue lolled out, his tail wagging.

The weather warmed, and shoots of green appeared. Geese and ducks flew overhead in droves, filling the world with their wild calls. I could not help but watch and scan the skies for each group, my heart pounding and my throat thick with longing for something I could not name.

The baby gave a squeak, and in our nest in the boat, I angled his cradleboard so that he might nurse. "Hear the geese, Little One. That is the sound of the changing of seasons. May you grow tall and live to witness many such migrations."

*****

Clark—April 1805

The babe enchanted us all. That tiny face, with the shock of black hair and dark eyes blinking at the sunlight—or simply watching—tended to so carefully by his young mother. Grown enough by the time we left to respond to smiles in kind. Providence grant they be kept safe, and that such new life among us bodes well for the journey.

Charbonneau told us the child was called *Jean Baptiste,* but someone dubbed him Little Pomp, and it stuck. His mama we took to calling *Janey* even though the name we were told she was called among the Minnetaree was *Sah-ca-ga-we-ah,* or Bird Woman, in their tongue.

Industrious, she was, from our very first day. When we stopped to make camp for the evening, she busied herself digging about under piles of driftwood, then brought us the fruits of her labor—a root resembling the Jerusalem artichoke in appearance and flavor, likewise good to eat, cached under the driftwood in large quantities by mice. When her explanation was translated, first through Charbonneau and then Jessaume, Lewis and I offered thanks, and when that was relayed back to her, she flashed us a shy smile which revealed charming dimples in both cheeks.

Just a few days later, we might have lost her and the babe. Charbonneau was steering the white pirogue and betrayed himself to be a mediocre waterman at best when a sudden squall of wind struck the sail and we tipped. In equally sudden alarm, Charbonneau turned the craft's side to the wind, further oversetting us. Lewis shouted for Drewyer, another Frenchman, to take in the sails. In short order, the pirogue was once again settled.

It was longer, I confess, before we could breathe easy. Lewis and I exchanged a long look. Thinking this the steadiest and safest of our boats, we'd packed all our instruments, papers, medicine, and the most valuable of our merchandise—not to mention the three men of our party who could not swim, the woman and baby, and ourselves.

I drew the air into my lungs, long and deep, and released it. Thank Providence we had escaped disaster.

Chapter Four

Sacagawea

The men's names grew more familiar to my ear. Lewis. Clark. York. Drewyer, of the same nation as my husband, well versed in the sign language of the Plains people. Labiche, whose task was to translate for my husband in place of Jessaume, the trader who had given Otter Woman the rattlesnake tail for me to drink. Cruzatte, who was very skilled at guiding the boats, and who sometimes played something called a *fiddle* that made the others very merry. Thirty men in all, and every one surprised me with their concern for me and the baby. Both leaders seemed to appreciate the bits of knowledge I could impart—though at this point it was little enough—but Clark made himself more easily approached, somehow. The smiles and even crooning over Little One, the warmth and interest in his gaze when I would bring roots or other foodstuffs to their meal preparations. I grew brave enough, while gathering at the edge of camp, to pluck the blossoms of a berry I recognized and offer it to him with instructions for gathering when ripe.

This last was conveyed through Drewyer, as Husband was too busy with cooking to bother with translating for me. Ever since our near disaster on that particularly cold and windy day, he had been even more stern and distant than usual, trying to prove himself before the white leaders as truly worthy. He did not forbid me to speak with the others, but it depended on his mood whether he thought my labors worthy or dismissed me.

Sometimes he would observe the concern shown me by the other men and then rush to make a show of doing the same. Of course all these things made him more attentive in other ways at the end of the day—although sometimes he did not wait until we were tucked into our bedroll at night, but would snatch moments when I was gathering.

sometimes not entirely out of sight of the other men. While he was demanding, he was also not over-harsh.

My only discontent was that were he a man of my own people, or even of the Minnetaree, he would be less likely to importune me while I had a nursing baby. But then, I was the only woman of the company, and Otter Woman was not present to meet that need for him.

A fear struck me, then—would he seek to barter me to the other men, as some husbands did?

I prayed his jealousy would at least keep him from that.

Such were the thoughts churning through my mind, keeping apace with the river on another blustery day. The winds blew cold and strong, which made the waters rough and caused me to nestle down amongst the luggage more snugly. As my husband took his turn guiding the boat, our leaders and some others walked the riverbank, the vessel again turned sideways and the waves nearly tipped us over. Cruzatte shouted at my husband, who suddenly seemed like a child who did not know what to do until Cruzatte pointed his small gun at him. But I could not think about that. I seized the side and braced myself with the baby strapped to my back, while the men fought to right the boat. This time, the water swept in and threatened to wash away our luggage, but I snatched all I could and tucked the bundles up next to me.

The boat at last was brought under control and to the shore. Clark and the others rushed over, babbling in what I thought to be mingled distress and relief.

After scolding my husband, Clark looked at me, gesturing to the baggage, his tone changing to one of admiration. I had done well, it seemed he said. I offered but a mild smile.

Anything more seemed—oh, immodest. And I did not know how Husband might react.

But my whole fortunes were bound up with these men. How could I not do what I was able, to save the baggage and all?

#

"I declare," Lewis said, his voice no less passioned for all that it was quiet, "the Indian woman possesses equal fortitude and resolution of any man on that pirogue."

As the sun set, we continued laboring to open all the parcels we'd salvaged and laid everything out to dry. We'd shouted ourselves hoarse, which neither Charbonneau nor Cruzatte paid any heed to—if they could hear us, so far were we onshore—and we witnessed Cruzatte pulling a gun on Charbonneau before the interpreter regained his own senses and brought the craft under control once more. Lewis afterward confessed he'd nearly given in to the temptation to attempt swimming out to them.

I sighed and stretched. "I heartily agree. Did you see her plucking parcels from the water, one handed?"

Lewis laughed. "As if she were just gathering roots, cool as you please." He stopped, looking about. "I fear our medicines sustained the greatest injury, and it remains to be seen on other things. But otherwise we only lost some garden seeds and a bit of our gunpowder, along with a few cooking items that likely lie on the bottom of the river."

Most of the parcels had been opened at this point, and the men dispersed to other tasks. The Indian woman tended her baby, singing softly as if, indeed, nothing amiss had occurred such a short time ago.

Chapter Five

Sacagawea

Of all things we could have eaten that evening, we feasted on bear. As the men finished unpacking all the things wetted by our near-spill, the sun having sunk out of sight, six of our number arrived in two canoes—being amongst those who brought up the rear of the group— with the creature they had killed and butchered. My husband, being much subdued by our fright with the pirogue tipping, gave me at least a short version of their adventure. Having seen the bear as they passed, they sought to sneak up on it and kill it, and shot it no fewer than eight times before it was finally overcome. I shuddered a little. Bears were amongst the most fearsome of animals, and the white men were brave— or a little out of their minds—to confront them as often as they did. But at least this encounter, as our own near disaster, ended well.

The next day, all was packed back up, accompanied by much muttering from our leaders. How I wished I could understand their speech! It would, I was sure, be very entertaining.

The next night, we were awakened with a shout and made to leave our lodge in the middle of the night. We rushed outside to find a large tree ablaze, we presumed from the sparks of our fire, and leaning over our lodge. The tree fell, but we escaped unhurt, with most of our goods undamaged.

A few days later I was informed, after stopping to explore one of the small rivers branching off the main one we traveled upstream on, that they had named it after me. *Sah-ca-ga-we-ah.* It was my Hidatsa name, not the one given by my Agai'dika mother, but a warm feeling filled me nevertheless at their regard. All the men smiled at me as if I had done something great. I smiled back, but uncertainly.

The country was changing as we traveled. A few trees grew along the river's edge, mostly evergreens and scrubby ones at that, and the surrounding land was more rugged and broken up, and very rocky. We caught glimpses of far-away hills and mountains. Not yet anything I recognized. I tucked away the longing that still fluttered in my heart.

*****

Clark—May-June 1805

What inhospitable country we had entered. Indeed, could anyone ever settle here and live?

I walked as often as I sailed, possibly more, scouting the lay of the land and surveying as far as I could see. York accompanied me and various others. Some commented on the strange beauty of the area—especially from the surrounding hilltops, into the distance—but I could only see the steepness of the bluffs, the lack of timber, the extreme dry barrenness of the ground here in what should be late spring or early summer. Having observed young along with the deer and elk for a little while already, we began to spy calves amongst the antelope as well.

The days were mostly uneventful, except that as the river narrowed and became more rapid, it became necessary to tow the canoes and pirogues upstream. Because of the ruggedness of the shore, sometimes the men made their way through chest-deep water, with mud and sharp rocks at the bottom making it both needful and yet impossible to continue wearing their moccasins. And on one night, we were awakened by an awful commotion—the sentry shouting, Lewis's dog Seaman barking furiously, and hooves thundering through the very center of our camp between the fires. A bull buffalo, spooked and stampeding. How any of us escaped being trampled, I do not know, for it passed within inches of sleeping men's heads.

That next day began the worst of the passage, towing the boats. At last we made it to the mouth of a slightly smaller river, pitched camp, and sent scouting parties upstream both ways.

We would stay here until we had surveyed the two rivers more completely.

Chapter Six

Sacagawea

What a barren land! The plains around the Minnetaree and Hidatsa were far more welcoming than this place.

There was a river the Minnetaree had told the white explorers about, which they called *River That Scolds At All Others.* This was not, I think, that stream yet. But it was difficult enough. I struggled to stay seated in the pirogue while the men towed it upstream, unable because of the rapids and riffles to sail, paddle, or even pole through. At least Little One stayed content enough because of the motion, and I had no real fear of my boat tipping, not even when the rope caught on the rocks and snapped, and the pirogue swung against the rocks. The men sprang into action to catch it again and bring it back.

When we reached the fork of a smaller river, camp was made where the ground was level enough to walk around comfortably. During hunting and foraging, though, the explorers startled a bear from its own foraging, and it chased my husband and Drewyer. Husband told me later that he had shot it but then had to hide deep in the brush to escape while Drewyer finished the kill.

Having bear to eat was always a good thing, though on this day we also had deer, elk, and other creatures from the men's hunting efforts. I did not want to contemplate what might happen to me if my husband perished on this journey, so I chose to thank Creator for his life being spared.

On another day, a bear attacked one of the men and might have killed him when his gun misfired, but the other men heard and ran to his rescue. They all shot at the bear and drove it away.

Every encounter made me shiver inside. Too well, I remembered how many men of my own people had sought to kill bears only to wind up a sacrifice to them instead, while those who took the creature gained honor equal to slaying a human enemy.

The men held much discussion. They moved the camp and split into groups to explore the area further. As the days wore on, however, I found myself simply weary. A bone-deep weariness that I pushed through for the sake of Little One. He would kick and wriggle and chortle while lying on a skin, free of his wrappings, still nursed with abandon, and grinned at any who stopped to admire him.

He truly was a joy. But oh, I was tired. And though I had escaped much of the illness that had befallen the others a few times, my belly was beginning to hurt.

*****

Clark—June 1805

We had explored enough, Lewis and I, to determine that the northernmost fork was not the Missouri. Lewis named it after his cousin Maria, and as we knew we were approaching the Great Falls of the Missouri, we determined to tie up our largest pirogue and cache many of our supplies for later. Our French *engages* knew this process so well, I left them to it.

Lewis would take a party and go further up the main river, while we prepared to go overland, above the Great Falls. A couple of days before he was to leave, he complained of being very unwell and of intestinal upset, so he dosed himself with salts. Toward evening of the day before his departure, however, we discovered our Indian woman to also be very unwell. I bled her, a usual treatment for sundry ailments, and she seemed a little better.

The next morning, Lewis felt unwell again but was determined to depart. He and his company set off upriver on foot, and the rest of us packed up the smaller pirogue and lighter canoes and set off on the water. I observed the Indian woman with uneasiness in my heart as she cared for the babe but listlessly. Charbonneau seemed to give her no heed. As the sun rose in the sky, I considered the heat of the bottom of the pirogue where we all sat and moved the woman and baby to the covered part of the pirogue where she at least might be shaded.

Many of the other men shared my concerns. The Indian woman had already been of such benefit to us, and what a great loss she would be as our only way of speaking with her people, who we hoped would help us cross over the great mountain range to the west. And her darling child—who would care for him if his mother died?

And how could we care for him? It wasn't as if we could milk the goats and antelope dwelling out on the plains.

So we tended her and gave Charbonneau directions for further watching her. On this second evening, he seemed a little less indifferent.

Each day we pushed further upriver. Once again we were reduced to towing the boats up the stream, with all of us wading and pulling, seeking footing over rocks that were alternately sharp and so smooth as to give us no purchase. The Indian woman lay in the pirogue under shade, not moving, the baby crying so long at times that it took Charbonneau shaking her to tend him. I could only grit my teeth at the callousness of his actions toward her, but there was little any of us could do in the moment. Carrying the babe on our backs, as the Indian woman did, was impracticable while we were engaged in towing the watercraft upstream.

Two days we did this, and on the second night, I took a short walk upstream to gauge the current and pitch of the water flow. Too close to the great falls for further travel on the river itself, we would have to seek portage around the falls from here. I sent Fields upstream on foot to find Lewis and inform him, then returned to camp.

We all passed a very uneasy night, with Sacagawea moaning and crying out in her sleep. I blinked into the darkness. What else could I do for her, besides bleeding, which had given her no relief the last time, or the decoction of Peruvian bark and laudanum, as I had been doing?

I thought of Charbonneau, wide eyed at the woman's refusal the day before to take any of the medicines I'd offered by mouth, begging us to go back downriver. I did not say so to his face, but what benefit would that be? We doubtless could not return to their former dwelling place in time to save her.

Lewis returned the next day about midmorning. Shock and concern lined his face as we looked in on the Indian woman, lying in the makeshift lodge Charbonneau had constructed for her, nearly out of her senses. He took her wrist, held it for a few moments, and shook his head. "I can hardly feel her pulse. And do you mark the twitching of her fingers and arm muscles?" He rose, looking around before meeting my gaze. "I will make a decoction of bark and laudanum, but I'm also determined to try waters from the sulfur springs we found." He sighed. "Would that I had more of the chokecherry decoction I made while out the first day, which cured me in a matter of hours."

"She may refuse to take any of that," I warned him, and told him of the previous day's experience.

He spread his hands in a gesture of helplessness. "We can but try."

Medicines prepared, we approached the woman again, where Charbonneau stood, holding the child and dandling him awkwardly. Lewis crouched beside the woman and spoke soothingly, trying to get her to take the medicine, but she still lay insensible.

We looked at each other, then at Charbonneau. Lewis gestured toward the cup he'd mixed, then the woman.

After a brief hesitation, Charbonneau held out the child, and I took him. The bright, dark eyes examined my bearded face with curiosity, one hand flailing toward me. "Hullo, little Pompey," I murmured.

Charbonneau knelt and spoke sharply to the woman, whose eyes fluttered, and when he supported her neck, consented at last to drink. She lay back with a long breath.

"Have you anything to feed the child with?" I mimed eating and pointed at the boy.

Charbonneau spread his hands as Lewis so recently had done. What, could the man not bestir himself to contribute to his own child's welfare?

"If they perish, it will be his fault," I muttered to Lewis.

"No doubt," he said, then rose. "I'll send someone to fetch the sulfur water now."

He returned within a couple of hours, repeating the process with the medicines. Sacagawea took it more willingly this time, and he pressed her to drink several small cupfuls of the mineral water.

"Now we wait," he said.

My own medical skills were not inconsiderable, but I found myself glad he had returned to help tend the woman. It would grieve me to lose her, and if her death were wholly on my watch? I did not think I could bear that.

Chapter Seven

Sacagawea

I awoke, as though surfacing through glittering water. Men's voices spoke near me, then further away. Was I yet in the realm of the living, or had I—would I—yet pass through to the spirit world, and join my ancestors and Creator? A great heaviness lay in my limbs, and an ache gnawed the lower part of my belly.

A baby cried. Oh—that was something I should be sensible to. A man's voice came then, again. "Wake, Bird Woman, and nurse our child." A heartbeat or three, then, "I ask you, wake, indeed."

I opened my eyes to find Husband bending over me, Little One in his hands, still weeping and so piteously that tears wet his tiny lashes. I sat, or rather half sat and rolled to my side, and bared a breast—which was so tight and full I could hardly bear touching it. Husband helped settle the baby against my side, and Little One's cries dissolved to mews of relief as he gladly latched on. The giving of milk hurt at first but also felt good. Felt right.

Husband moved away a little, watching with a look I could not interpret. Was he angry? Glad? I fed the child on one side and eased over to the other, closing my eyes against the dark gaze of the bearded man I had belonged to for the past year and more.

"Are you feeling any better?" he asked.

His words surprised me. I peered over at him, squinting.

"You have been sick. Very sick."

"How many suns?"

He counted on his fingers. "Five or six." He offered the barest smile. "It is hard to feed our son without your milk."

As our child fell asleep, still nursing, the one called Lewis approached again and spoke.

"He asks if you feel more well and where you still have pain."

I considered, and swept a hand side to side across my lower belly. Lewis nodded, and taking my wrist, pressed his fingers against my pulse for a few breaths before nodding again more strongly, with a smile.

Clark approached behind him, eyes crinkling as he studied me, then also offered a nod.

The sun was going down, and once more I slept, though not with the feeling this time that I would pass on to the next world at any moment. Come morning, Lewis brought me what he called *soop,* made by the seething of meat in water with whatever roots and plants they saw fit to add. I sipped—and it tasted good. I smiled my thanks.

This was the seventh day, I discovered, since I had fallen ill. The men feared for my life. They all filed by to watch me drink soop and nibble at the tender, seasoned buffalo that Lewis had directed prepared for me, to offer smiles and nods and chuck my little one under the chin to see him laugh. It warmed me to see it all. Husband's smile grew rather thin by the end of the day. Lewis gave him a long speech at one point, pointing to me and my food, speaking most earnestly, and Husband bobbed his head but said nothing else.

During all this, preparations were being made, I learned, for making yet another cache of supplies, for we would be traveling on foot until past the falls. My heart beat a little faster. I knew of this area. And it seemed—perhaps—that we would be traveling in truth toward my people the Agai'dika.

I forced myself to calmness. It had not yet happened. And there was no guarantee we would find anyone of my immediate family. I had watched the Minnetaree slaughter some of them that fateful day they took me, after all.

\#

Clark
I could not adequately express my happiness at seeing the Indian woman awake, taking nourishment, and free of fever or pain. Once

again I could tuck aside the thought of the unhappy circumstance we had faced with her near death.

I left early the next morning with five men and five of the lighter canoes to be carried upstream, overland. The falls were nothing if not beautiful, but our way proved so treacherous, I nearly slipped and tumbled to what almost certainly would have been my own death.

As it was, we all narrowly escaped more times than we could count. Lewis related how, while returning from surveying the great falls, he was attacked first by a bear, then a wildcat, then by three bull buffalo. How he escaped, he was not sure, but he left behind a buffalo he had just brought down, feeling it unwise to stay the night in such an area. Just days later, while taking my own turn scouting, I slipped and fell into a deep pool on the river and only by much effort escaped drowning.

We were not praying men, as some, but there were days it seemed some greater hand did indeed hold and preserve us. *Providence,* my elders would have called it, as I also did by habit, without thinking overlong on what that truly meant.

Perhaps it was something to which I should give more attention.

Chapter Eight

Sacagawea

Day by day, I grew stronger. On the second day, I walked out to gather roots, which tasted so good I ate too many, along with some dried fish, and wound up with a gut ache again. Lewis scolded my husband, who shrugged and pointed at me, but I had not been told not to eat these things. Lewis looked very angry but dealt tenderly enough with me when he dosed me with his strange medicines, and my fever broke again about evening with a fine sweat.

The next day, I felt well enough to walk up and down the river and to fish. Clark and his party returned a day or two after, and he greeted me heartily, then the men set to their plans to move some of the baggage upstream. Clark and Lewis and most of the men left, with my husband and the black man York remaining with me. I was glad I need not travel just yet.

Back and forth they went, Lewis returning first, then leaving again, then Clark returning, and preparations began in earnest. The men also worked on mending their moccasins and adding a layer to the sole, as well as making new ones, for the roughness of the ground we were to face would quickly wear them out. Husband directed me to do the same with both his and mine, explaining that the prickly pear grew thick on our way and had proved most troublesome to those who had already journeyed that direction. I nodded, remembering well from my childhood.

Finally it was our turn to go up the stream along the falls. Husband and I were out strolling with Clark, the others carrying the load not far away, when a very threatening cloud came up. Clark eyed it with some alarm, then led my husband and I down into a ravine, where we took refuge under an overhang of rock just as the rain began. And what a rain it was! Falling in sheets, pounding the earth, with chunks of ice also falling.

Scarcely had I unbundled Little One to change and feed him—it had been too long since I had taken time for that—when Clark gave a shout and my husband as well. I looked up to see water pouring down the side of the hill, with rocks and dirt heading into our hiding spot. Husband scrambled upward despite the rain and water falling. I snatched Little One into my arms and ran, Clark all but carrying us toward the wall. He gestured, but I needed not his direction to understand.

We had to leave this place or perish.

One handed, I scrambled for foot- and handholds. Husband tried clumsily to help me from above. Clark pushed from behind. Creator— oh Creator!

Somehow we made it up to the face of the cliff and over the edge, one by one, to where York was searching furiously for us. I sat, huddled around Little One, breathing hard, but Clark plucked me up by the shoulders and half carried me to where we had left the rest of the party.

I collapsed next to one of the canoes, drawing Little One in to nurse. Clark put a buffalo skin about me, warm and dry, and spoke soothingly, before turning away to speak to the others. They straggled in, all wet and muddy as we were, some with clothing shredded and some bleeding from the violence of the hail.

What a storm we had survived.

I had nothing left of my baby's belongings, I realized. The cradleboard, his clothing and bedding—all left behind and doubtless lost.

But our lives . . . we had our lives.

*****

Clark

We had all survived that wild storm.

112

The other men, most caught out in the open, had suffered being not just buffeted by the wind but by hail as well, some knocked down, some wounded, some nearly killed. I passed out a dram of liquor from York's canteen, and we all sipped at it, catching our breath, gathering our spirits. Around the fire that night, we reflected on the mercy of Providence that we were yet living and breathing.

The next day, we packed everything as best as we could—I'd dug into our stores to clothe and furnish little Pomp again, and Janey seemed grateful—and set out. We made it without incident to the upper portage camp, where Lewis was hard at work with his experiment of a boat with an iron frame, carefully wrought to his specifications, covered over with animal skins and thoroughly pitched. When placed on the water, however, the flaws in the concept soon became apparent, though it initially floated like a cork. Lewis pointed to a portion covered in buffalo skins, where he had merely singed off the hair rather than scraping it. "See how this holds the water perfectly? If only I had treated the elk skins the same way, it might have entirely held."

"What now?" I asked him, though I knew the answer.

Lewis raked a hand through his hair, even longer and more shaggy than when we had first set out. "This is by necessity the end of my experiment. It would be madness to continue trying to make it work. Though I confess myself very impatient to keep going on our journey. I cannot see how we might succeed in getting to the ocean and back and to Fort Mandan this season."

We agreed I would go a little upstream and to the other shore to seek trees for making more canoes. That part of the endeavor took us nearly two weeks, but we had a pair of canoes ready, each made from a tree, by the time Lewis and the others joined us.

Chapter Nine

Sacagawea

As we ascended the river southward each day, we grew closer. I could feel it. And still I did not allow myself to hope.

The cactus began to bloom, adding beauty to the region, despite its menace to our feet when we had to walk. Various berries ripened, which all the men appreciated. Little One burbled and cooed often, except when he was hungry. I was thankful that my milk had not failed during the week I was sick.

I tired more easily than before, but did my best not to show it.

And then, just a handful of days after we had set out again, we encountered a section of the river where the channels wove through a series of islands. Lewis left the canoes to go upland and survey the river from above, while I found myself hanging nearly overboard to examine the trees and land. Mountain goats leaped nimbly up the faces of tall cliffs rising on either side of the river. Ground squirrels scurried at the water's edge as we passed.

Yes. Yes, I was sure. I asked Husband to tell our leaders we were nearing the area where my people lived. We were also very close to the spot where the main river branched into three smaller ones, as they had been told by the Minnetaree.

The next day, Clark selected men to accompany him on foot, and my husband begged to go along. Clark looked at me before answering. Was he thinking of the possible use I would be if we encountered my people? Or concerned I would hinder them with my fatigue and the need to care for the baby? I could not tell.

At last, Husband departed with Clark and I stayed with the main party, so the baby and I could be as comfortable as possible in the canoes. I contented myself with the situation the best I could, pointing out things and communicating by signs and gestures when needed.

Then one morning, the men poled us upriver until we came to a wide, green meadowy expanse where the waters split various ways. My heart beat hard within my chest. Lewis exclaimed, and the canoes were drawn up to a particularly lush area where exploration on foot began, and the men set up to stay awhile. I found shade and settled in to tend Little One. After he was fed and tucked snugly in the deer hide I had fashioned to sling him at my back in the absence of the cradle board, I made my own cautious explorations.

There was no sign of my people here now, but too well I remembered what this place represented for us.

At this moment, however, I had no one to tell. No one I could share it with.

Relief of a mixed sort seeped through me when Clark and my husband and the other men rejoined us a few hours later. Clark was ill this time. Husband had twisted his ankle and limped, but it was Clark's life I feared for. I could see in the faces of York and Lewis that they too were concerned. I watched, holding back a little as they tended him, even while I halfheartedly offered ministrations to my own husband. His ankle did not appear to be broken despite terrible bruising, and I told him he should go soak it in the river. He grumbled at me, but did take himself to the river's edge.

The next morning found both him and Clark a little better. Lewis had an awning set up to afford Clark some shade. Other men were busy laying out all their belongings for a thorough drying—water often splashed over the sides of the canoes and wet us all down—and others were busy making more clothing and moccasins. I had scraps with which to replenish Little One's clothing and wraps, but kept looking around, waiting, listening.

I should tell them. But somehow I could not bring myself to do so, just yet.

#

"I have felt better, I confess." I covered my face with my arm as I lay back on the driest of our baggage under the cover Lewis had caused to be set up for me.

An understatement, at best. My very bones still ached, and a chill lay upon me from the lingering fever. A brief thundershower had cooled the air, which the other men greatly appreciated, but I could not help but think of that day I'd been caught out and unprepared with Charbonneau and his wife and child.

At the thought, my gaze sought them. Charbonneau still limped but worked shoulder to shoulder with the hunters who had recently returned, helping clean and skin their take and prepare both for immediate cooking and dressing the skins on the morrow.

"I am told," Lewis said, seeing where my attention strayed, "that our interpreter nearly met his demise."

I nodded shortly. "The current in the river was so swift, and the pocket so deep, he was almost swept away. I merely reached in and pulled him out."

A smile played about Lewis's mouth. "I am told you did more than merely reaching in—that you risked your own life saving his."

I shrugged, and it hurt to do so.

"And you being unwell, at that," Lewis murmured. His gaze also strayed, and he sighed deeply. "Surely we must soon reach the Snake people."

"Surely," I grunted.

The Indian woman caught my eye then. Something about her seemed amiss, but she labored just as much as any of the men. Not that we expected anything different.

Lewis patted my shoulder. "I shall return."

Supper seemed a merry enough affair. And then, in the midst of the men sitting about and talking, Charbonneau abruptly loomed over me, Janey at his elbow. He spoke, and Jessaume moved closer and made him repeat the matter before turning to me. "He says the Indian woman has aught to tell you."

I propped myself a little higher against a stack of baggage and bid them continue. She looked at Charbonneau, then me, then spat out a sentence, all in a rush.

Charbonneau to Labiche, then—"She says we are camped on the exact spot where her people made camp the day she was taken by the Minnetarees."

I did sit up at that. Several of the men around us exclaimed, then leaned closer. "Captain Lewis!" I called. "You will want to make note of this."

He drew near, and the matter was repeated. As he scrambled for writing materials, the woman said something again, almost under her breath, weaving on her feet.

Once more, the tedium of translation. "She says it may not be of interest to you at all, and the telling is slow . . ."

"Oh no, we are most certainly interested," Lewis said.

"And this is good practice for translation with her people," I added.

Bit by bit, the story came out.

Five years ago—she was only eleven summers—her people had camped here to seek the buffalo as their custom every year. The Minnetarees attacked, and her people fled some, oh, we gauged it three miles or so up the river we had named the Jefferson. They hid in the trees, but the Minnetarees hunted them. Many were killed—four men, four women, several boys. All the other women and young girls were taken captive, along with some of the boys, and taken back to their dwelling on the Knife River.

She was one of those.

I watched her while she spoke. So calm, so composed. "Too composed," Lewis said later. "I can see no emotion whatsoever in her, neither sorrow for being a captive nor joy for seeing her people again. It is as if she is content with having enough to eat and a few trinkets to wear, and that is that."

I hummed with thought. "I am not sure I agree with your assessment on this." Something about her manner bespoke of deep emotion, perhaps too much.

Lewis raised one brow in my direction. "Oh?"

I shrugged again. "We will see once we actually find her people."

Chapter Ten

Sacagawea

Husband demanded my attentions that evening, so it was late before I could leave Little One sleeping and slip away alone—and even then, not too far, because the threat of bears was still very much too present. But I needed solitude—to remember, to cry, to mourn all I had lost.

Only a moment, of course. Tucked between two of the canoes, I stopped my almost-silent sobbing long enough to hear the approach of one of the men, and I lay quiet and unmoving until he passed. I dared not linger further. Back at the side of my husband and child, tears leaked out of my eyes for a long time, unhindered, though I made no other sound.

By the next day, I was able to be calm in the presence of the men.

Clark was a little better. Husband only complained of some soreness in his limbs, and his own ankle was improving. Lewis directed the men to load the canoes, and we continued up the river, with Husband and I and a couple of other men who were unwell walking. A fair distance farther, I was nearly overcome at finding and pointing out the spot where the Minnetaree found and took me. Onward we went.

On the second day, Lewis prepared to set out to find my people, and once again my husband begged to go. After much discussion, Lewis gave in, while I was left with the main party, led by Clark, who was recovering but slowly.

Much of this portion was on foot. Having come to yet another fork in the river, Clark chose the westernmost branch, and though the men were able to pole the canoes in some places, others were so rocky and steep, with small waterfalls, they were forced to tow the canoes. I insisted on getting out and walking.

Was this portion of the river familiar? I could not decide. Anticipation gnawed at me as I climbed rocky slopes, sometimes nearly on my hands and knees.

Lewis returned after several days, just as things were going even worse for the men towing the canoes. Three had already spilled.

While he and Clark discussed the problem of wet baggage and the awful, oozing swelling that had developed on Clark's ankle, I walked around a little and looked up to see a very familiar outline amongst the mountaintops surrounding us.

It was none other than Beaverhead Mountain! I knew we were close now—very close—and I ran to tell our leaders. Lewis laughed a little at the name of it, called so because of its resemblance to the head of that animal, but he considered the mountain with a look of longing.

The next day he was off again, leaving Clark to manage the canoes. I could tell it was not a task that pleased him.

At supper, I sought to soften things for him, and gave him a slightly larger portion of the roots I had discovered, sparse though they were overall. He smiled and thanked me, and though I only gave a nod, I turned to see Husband glaring at me. I dropped my gaze and went about my next task, which was to feed Little One some of the root.

Another handful of days passed. Drewyer returned to give us the news that Lewis had met some of the Indian people, and from what he could tell, they were of the Agai'dika.

Every breath stirred hope and felt like the edge of a knife inside my throat.

The land leveled somewhat, and the river was full of shoals. The men continued hauling the canoes but with even more difficulty than before. Everyone was weary. Clark spoke to them, and they seemed to gain strength from his words.

They labored thus for the next four days. On the fifth we rose early and were not long set out when Drewyer appeared with the news that he, Lewis, and the others had indeed found the people they sought, were welcomed by them, and even now were on their way to meet up with us, accompanied by many of the people. My heart beat so fast I could hardly breathe, and if I had not already accomplished my morning's tasks of dressing, putting my hair in order, and feeding and bundling Little One, my fingers could not have held steady to do so now.

Clark immediately took Husband and I, and with Drewyer we set out to meet them ahead of the canoes.

I thought of my friend who had succeeded in escaping the Minnetarees not long after we had been taken by them. What had befallen her? Had she reached our people?

I would soon find out.

We heard them a little before they came into sight—the sound of horses 'hooves and snorts, the chatter of women woven through that of the men. I swallowed and tried to steady my limbs. One foot in front of the other . . .

And then—there they were. The familiar mode of dress, the horses so proud and graceful—for a moment the sight stole my breath entirely.

How beautiful they all were—but how thin and lean—yet how lovely!

A cry burst from my throat. I jumped up and down, then danced around my husband. "There! There they are, my people!"

Their exclamations and songs split the morning air as they likewise rejoiced to see us. Another woman's cry came to my ear, and who should be running toward me but my own friend.

I met her halfway, and we embraced, laughing and weeping at once. "Oh, I hoped it was you!" she exclaimed. "And such a sweet baby! You are also a mother now, as I am."

We hugged again, then I stepped back to look at her. "You made it all that way?"

Tears ran down her face, and she nodded, grinning. "I did. I will tell you all later, but they now call me Poppank for how I went through the water to escape the Minnetaree."

Jumping Fish. How fitting.

"I am now called Sacagawea, or Bird Woman in the speech of the Minnetaree."

"So we were told by the white men."

The other women surrounded us then, repeating their own names in case I had forgotten—or that theirs had changed in the five turns of the seasons we had been apart. They exclaimed over Little One and told of their own children, all of which had been left behind at their camp on the westward-flowing river in case we had turned out to be enemies. Though we laughed at that, I knew it had been a wise decision. Too easily that could have been the case.

At last, when I could collect myself again and look around, I was both surprised and gratified to see both Clark and Lewis watching with smiles upon their faces.

The other canoes arrived as the sun stood overhead. They busied themselves making camp and setting up awnings to sit under and talk. The real work would begin later in the afternoon. I would sit with my husband and Labiche, and as Clark or Lewis would speak, Labiche would translate to my husband, who would translate to me, and then I to my people.

When they were ready, my husband interrupted my conversation with the women. "You are wanted at council to help translate now."

It was the reason I had been brought, of course. Quickly I told the women what he had said. They nodded and eyed him as Poppank took Little One and motioned me to go do what was needed.

I followed him to where a shelter had been made of willow branches, a welcome shade in the midst of a warm day. A white buffalo skin was laid down, and all the men had removed their moccasins before they began the solemn task of passing around the pipe. I also slipped off my shoes and sat down to begin my task.

Lewis was speaking and Labiche translating to my husband when I looked at the chief present—truly looked—and recognized him. Another cry tore from my throat. "My brother! My own brother!"

Older than me by a few years, and made too lean by the poverty they had suffered because of the Minnetaree attacks, but it truly was him. He accepted my tearful, exuberant embrace and embraced me in return. "My little sister, returned to us after all this time."

Cameahwait, he was called. *One Who Never Walks,* so named for his position, which allowed him to go on horseback everywhere. And indeed, he had become chieftain.

I took a deep breath, to calm my once-again racing heart, and began. How I wanted this to go well for all involved.

Lewis began by explaining the size of their country and government and all the things our people could gain by allying themselves with the white men and by aiding them in their journey. He explained in much detail what they hoped to accomplish in the journey, and how no trade could happen until they had succeeded in going all the way to the ocean and back to report to their leaders.

He also emphasized that they did not ask for horses or any other assistance without the intent to compensate my people adequately. Cameahwait appeared well pleased by all that was said.

Afterward, my friend Poppank brought Little One to me to nurse. "You did not tell me my brother had become chieftain," I said.

Her smile held a proud edge, dark eyes sparkling.

I gasped. "Are you—"

"Yes. I am his wife. Or rather, one of them."

"I am so happy! You are my sister indeed, now!"

Sadness edged her face then. "He and another brother are all that is left of your family—the other is away at the moment. And then there is a young boy, the son of your oldest sister, who is also dead."

I bowed my head, giving in to the tears wholly. "I—had hoped—"

Her arms came around me and Little One. "I am your sister now. And you have come back to us, even if only for a short time."

Chapter Eleven

Sacagawea

The white men threw a feast with deer the hunters had brought in, then spent much time displaying and demonstrating what they had brought along. York caused much wonder, as did Lewis's great furry dog. When Lewis shot one of his guns, all my people broke out in loud exclamations and cries, and I had to laugh even as I reassured them.

At one time it had all been new and strange to me as well.

It was decided that Cameahwait would take our people and return to their village on the westward flowing river, over the ridge from this one, and my husband and I would accompany them to assist in their preparations for furnishing us with horses.

When we had a chance, I sidled up to my brother.

Brother! Who was chieftain!

"What do you think of the white men and their ideas?" I asked.

He stood with folded arms, watching a contest between Shoshone and white man. "I will do what is best for our people. And if their ideas can help us, then—" He shrugged.

I nodded.

"That white man who is your husband," Cameahwait said. "Are you content with him?"

I had to think on my reply. "Content enough."

"Rises-With-The-Sun said he would consider pressing his claim as your husband."

A little jolt, not entirely unpleasant, went through me.

How would I feel about being free of Charbonneau? All things considered, he had not been so terrible. He made sure I had plenty of hides for clothing and enough blue beads to make a belt and decorate my fittings.

"Or do you wish to stay with these men and see the ocean where the sun sets, as well?" Cameahwait's eyes gleamed.

"It is not like that," I snapped.

He chucked almost soundlessly. "Like what?"

"Like—what you seem to believe."

He sniffed. "Were I free, I might want to go as well. But I warn you, if you thought the journey here difficult, the way from here will be even more so."

I made myself to breathe in, then out, evenly. "If I stay, will my life will be any better?"

He was quiet, then, "It may be, but it may not. We only had cakes of dried berries to feed our guests, much to my shame, and they fed us with meat. So, you judge."

I did not know how to feel about any of it. There was something to be said of staying—rejoining my people, and letting Little One grow to manhood here. My husband would be unhappy about it, of course . . . not that he could do much about a prior betrothal.

Whether that prior betrothal could actually hold, however, I also did not know. Would Rises-With-The-Sun even still want me?

*****

That, at least, I discovered rather quickly.

We were sitting around the fire that very evening, mostly finished with the feasting, when an Agai'dika warrior stood and approached Cameahwait. A chill went through me as I recognized him. Strong and tall, well into his manhood. Handsome in a severe way. His eyes swept me before he came to a halt before my brother. "I have come to speak concerning my betrothal to your sister. Your father promised her to me many years ago, but she had not yet come of age before the Minnetaree took her."

Cameahwait seemed unbothered by his demand. "She is now of age, but do you not have two other wives? And she had been given to another man—the one named Charbonneau, who travels with the other white men."

He bobbed his head, looking a little uncertain.

My husband pushed forward. "What is happening?"

I rose to stand beside him, bouncing Little One in my arms. "I was promised as wife to this one when I was still a child," I told him quietly as Rises-With-The-Sun's gaze caught on the child, then on Charbonneau. "He has come to make good on that promise."

Charbonneau exclaimed, then babbled something in his own speech. I held up a hand to stop him. "Let us see how the matter will play out first."

To my amazement, he held his tongue, though he looked furious.

Clark and Lewis also stood near, suddenly, both frowning.

I turned to Rises-With-The-Sun. "Will you also take my child?"

He seemed to consider, first Little One, then me, then the glowering man at my side. "I would have taken you to wife, even though I have two women. Yet since you have borne his child"—he made a dismissive motion with his fingers—"I do not want you."

Something in his dark eyes belied the words, but I dipped my head to accept his statement. And strangely, mingled disappointment and relief rushed through me like the river rapids.

"So be it, then," Cameahwait said.

I sat down again, but our white leaders would not rest until they had learned everything. Lewis, especially, I knew had a great curiosity about all things—birds and animals and their differences, and the ways of various peoples. He questioned me about Agai'dika marriage customs and many other things. Through all of it, Husband did not cease looking angry until Lewis was satisfied and he and the other men had gone away, leaving us to retire for the night.

"You are my woman, and no one else's," he said.

I nodded.

"Would you have chosen to stay?"

I considered how to answer those sharp words. Would he have done violence to keep me, had Rises-With-The-Sun maintained his claim?

"I am your woman," I said simply.

Why would he ask such a thing? When had I ever been given a choice?

Chapter Twelve

Clark—August 1805

I observed the anger of Charbonneau and could not help but hover near in case the man broke out in violence, either against the Shoshone warrior who had stood up to state his claim upon Sacagawea or against Sacagawea herself.

"The man is more than twice her age," Lewis protested under his breath.

I merely grunted. Did he not understand the way of things? My own Julia, who I hoped to wed—or Judy as her family called her—was roughly that, to me. And who knew the true age of Charbonneau?

But perhaps it betrayed a tenderness Lewis had developed for the Indian woman, a tenderness I could only be sympathetic to.

"Charbonneau looks near ready to strike her," Lewis went on.

"He did, but three nights ago," I said.

Lewis rounded on me. "What?"

I shrugged but still felt anything but diffident about it. "I had gone hunting and brought back a buck and a fawn. I gave her the skin from the fawn, for little Pomp or however she chose to use it. She thanked me so effusively, Charbonneau glowered at her after. He scolded her while they were sitting at supper. Whatever her response to that, it did not please him, for he struck her. I rebuked him sharply for it, but you know Charbonneau."

Lewis grimaced, and a growl rose from him.

"But on a lighter note, I told you the situation would be different amongst her people." I nudged Lewis with an elbow.

"So you did."

All afternoon we had both witnessed the Indian woman's exuberant joy, one moment chattering with the other women, in the next, heads together with her friend, admiring little Pomp and laughing over his grins.

*****

Sacagawea

In the coming days, Husband and I returned with the Agai'dika to help speed our purchase of horses. Clark went exploring for a clear route westward. Lewis dickered with Cameahwait over the moving of baggage, and when it became clear that we would need horses for a greater part of our journey, over how many the Agai'dika could spare.

In the meantime, because game was scarce, my people showed the white men how to build a fishing weir, and together they made one that spanned the whole river. We caught many fish that day and enjoyed the first of many feasts.

They exclaimed over our favorite, which they called *salmon* but we called agai. I pointed to the fish—*agai*—and mimed eating it—*dika*—and tried to convey to Clark and Lewis that this was my people's true name. At least they no longer called us the Snake people, which had been a misunderstanding of the hand sign of a fish swimming, but *Shoshoni.*

One morning while strolling about, I overheard my brother and other chiefs discussing their intent to depart soon for the headwaters of the eastward-flowing river for a last attempt at buffalo hunting before winter. My heart beat hard as I considered whether or not to share this information. I knew from our talks with Cameahwait that he had promised, and Lewis fully expected, that he would furnish the expedition with horses, first to carry their baggage over the mountain ridge and then north and over the rest of the mountains.

The choice had been made for me, I reminded myself, when Rises-With-The-Sun made to claim and then rejected me. So, to my husband I went and shared what I had heard. He nodded, but all day I watched

129

and waited without any sign that he had conveyed it to Lewis. Finally I could not wait, and I pestered him about it.

I could tell the exact moment it happened, however. Husband went to Lewis, almost casually, and spoke as if they were discussing the weather. Lewis exclaimed and, after a long scold at my husband, demanded a meeting with my brother.

After observing every formality he knew, including smoking a pipe with my brother and the other two chiefs before beginning his speech, Lewis had me ask whether they did not intend to honor their own word. My brother avowed that yes, they did indeed. Why then, Lewis asked, were they sending for other peoples to meet them over on the Missouri for a hunt rather than helping us move our baggage? Cameahwait's gaze slid my way. He knew where Lewis had gained his information. I held myself still, but my gut felt hollow.

My brother said it was not that he did not intend to fully follow through on his word and then begged concern for our people. "We are poor and starving because of the afflictions laid on us by the Minnetaree. We need this meat to survive the winter."

"That is understandable," Lewis said. "Yet we cannot help make your lives better until we can complete our journey and return to the east, and we need your help to accomplish that."

Much conversation had already taken place regarding other peoples, north and south and westward, the Pierced Noses and others. Clark returned and confirmed, as Cameahwait had said, that there would be no passage downstream on the greater river that adjoined the one where the Agai'dika currently dwelled—the water was too swift, the mountainsides too steep and treacherous. But the Pierced Noses used a path leading north from our valley, up over the mountains, then turning to the west. It was difficult, Cameahwait warned, but Clark and Lewis were determined that if the Pierced Noses could manage it, with women and children along, our company would indeed do the same.

When all our preparations were complete, we set out on that northward path, each of us on our own horse with extra horses to carry baggage and provide spares. Our way was rugged and treacherous in places—at least one horse and rider fell, but none came to serious harm. Not many days passed before the horror of having no food occurred—the hunters could neither find nor bring down any meat—and the decision was made to eat one of the young horses. I wept many bitter tears over that but could not refuse the opportunity to eat as well. My child and I must live, whatever that meant. We had already been reduced more than once to eating dogs, as poor as that was. How I longed, all over again, for the tender flesh of roasted agai, the fish for which our people were named.

I would not let myself think about how, if Rises-With-The-Sun had insisted on keeping me, I would not, perhaps, have to eat horse.

We did make it over the mountains, whose peaks rising above us lay clothed in white even in the heat of summer, and into the valley beyond where the bitterroot flower grew. There we could gather quamash roots, and other things. The men found it indifferent at best, but at least it was food. The mountains towered above us as we turned westward and pressed into the heart of those beautiful but unforgiving peaks.

I was grateful to have my own horse with Little One strapped securely to my back. And not just any horse, half worn out, but a good one. I knew Lewis had given my husband special trade goods to make sure this was the case.

Husband had sulked about it, but he did as Lewis instructed.

After reaching the valley to the north, we encountered the Salish people and enjoyed a peaceful encounter with them. Then it was time to tackle the path westward.

Chapter Thirteen

Almost ten days followed of the most perilous riding, through the hardest country. There had been frost in the high country where my people dwelt, but the cold deepened even more. We woke one morning with our robes covered in snow, and the mountainsides were so rough in places that several horses fell, including my husband's mount. When I watched Clark and Lewis in the evening, trying to write accounts of the days, I could see that it was tedious for them. They stared at their papers, passing a hand through their hair, and sighing while rubbing the backs of their necks.

I felt more than a little useless. With no berries and very few roots for me to forage, there was not much for me to contribute to the overall wellbeing of these men I accompanied.

Despite the cold and hunger, despite the treacherous paths, we made it over the mountains and soon met up with the people called the Pierced Noses, or *Chopunnish* in their own speech, and bargained for a little food and more horses. I thought myself of no use here as well, since I could not speak their tongue and my own people were long behind us. But the people of the village were full of caution and unwilling to come out to greet us until I stepped forward, Little One in full view on my back, and suddenly they were all friendliness.

This proved so wherever we went, even after we gave up horses for canoes—a few of which the men made and a few we had traded for. And I believe in more than one case, my presence kept the warriors of any particular people from slaying all the white men on the spot. I was truly, as a woman and mother with her child, proof that their intentions were of peace and not war. I felt humbled by this, yet proud at the same time, and grateful once more to the Creator. For the first time since we left my people I felt it might be of some good that I had stayed with the expedition.

Traveling downriver—now that was a change, and an adventure. Riding with the rapids rather than pulling against them, watching the shoreline slide past with its richness of plant and animal life. We slipped past more mountains and hills, some every bit as rugged as those we had walked and ridden through.

How different were the people as we went. As a child, I had met some of the Salish, Chopunnish, and even the Flat Heads with their strange way of molding their babies 'heads into a sloped point that they thought attractive, but those closer to the great sea—why, the women wore hardly any covering at all, just a band front to back, tied to a strap about their waists. As we neared the sea, even that was dispensed with in favor of a short tunic of animal skins and a skirt made of fluttering strips of bark.

Why it should surprise me, I did not know. And it wasn't as if the women of any nation did not in some way or another make their favors available to the men of the expedition, particularly the younger ones. I knew from conversations with the Minnetaree women that they did it partly for courtesy, partly the novelty of being with a white man, and partly for the small objects they were given in exchange. Regardless, all suffered for it, some more than others. I saw by gesture that Lewis gave out medicines and advice for treating the sores that often flared up on the other men after enjoying local hospitality.

It also seemed that the peoples farther west were as poor as the Agai'dika, possibly more so, and less generous with what they did have. Husband told me that many of them were already accustomed to trading with white men who came in ships over the ocean and landed on the western coast we were nearing.

The year grew later, it was clear, but the weather was not so cold as to snow. Still, as we traveled farther downriver, it rained and rained, and we were seldom dry. I had never felt such a thing in all my life.

At last came the day when, despite the misery of rain and not being able to find a good campsite—many of the old villages were infested by fleas—we could glimpse what Clark, Lewis, and the others called *oh-shen*. The river as we knew it widened to a bay, where on stormy days great waves washed in from the sea, and even on calmer days the roaring of those waves at the mouth of the bay was constant.

Groups of local peoples came and went, anxious to have a look at us. None could speak their tongue, but Drewyer and others managed basic communication with sign. They examined everyone and everything, including details of my own dress, tattered though it was now, and the belt of blue beads I still wore about my waist.

During the time the men were still discussing where to make a permanent camp for the winter, one such group visited, whose chief wore an admittedly gorgeous otter-skin coat. I had not seen either Clark or Lewis so taken with an item before, although Lewis had been given a short cape made of otter skin and weasel tails by my people, the Agai'dika, which he seemed very fond of.

Clark offered for this coat, only to be refused. Lewis joined in. The dickering went back and forth, during which the man who wore it kept casting me glances. A chill touched me. I did not think I wanted to know what he had in mind.

At last Lewis turned to us, motioning to Labiche for his assistance in speaking to my husband. His answer at first was a firm shake of the head, but his gaze was not so much on me as on—my middle. Specifically, that blue beaded belt I had labored over and now wore.

My fingers went to the item, gently tracing the beadwork.

Another round of talk commenced between the local man with the otter-skin coat, Drewyer, Lewis, Clark, and Labiche. Husband's mouth thinned, and his eyes flicked to mine. "He is willing to trade that coat for your belt," he said, confirming what I had finally gathered.

A breath in, a breath out. My fingers fumbled at first with the ties, but I would comply with the request, if only for my regard for Clark.

That one spoke, a little more urgently, and it was passed through Labiche and my husband, who seemed embarrassed. "He says he will gladly repay you in blue beads to make a new one once we have returned eastward."

I nodded and finished untying the belt. Draping it across one arm, I held it out to Clark.

His dark eyes met mine, a little abashed but grateful. He gave me a short bow, and I nodded in return as he lifted the belt from my arm.

I did not want to stay and watch the rest of the transaction, but courtesy and custom held my feet rooted to the place where I stood.

*****

Clark—November 20, 1805

I had not intended to take anything off of Janey's own person for this trade, much less that blue belt she so obviously treasured. But the matter seemed taken out of my hands.

York stood by with an inscrutable look on his face, which usually meant he disapproved but of course dared say nothing. Even Lewis had the good grace to look ashamed. "You *will* repay her," he said, very low, as I rejoined him.

"Of course," I murmured.

As the Indian handed over the otter-skin coat, crowing over the blue belt, I glanced at Janey. She now gazed steadfastly at the ground. It struck me then how very much we owed her—how much I owed her— in so many ways.

From the beginning, we had tried to shield her from much of the hardship, from initially housing her and Charbonneau and the babe in our own lodge, to ensuring her comfort in the pirogues, and that she had a good horse to carry her and little Pomp over the mountains. Now, it seemed woefully inadequate.

York steadfastly refused to meet my eye for days, even after I gave her a coat of blue cloth in payment. It was too late to go back on the transaction—not that the Indian would have given up his prize in those blue beads—and I could not even offer Janey the otter-skin coat, lest Charbonneau see it as untoward favoritism. So I was stuck.

In the coming weeks, however, I tried to show her deference in small ways. One was when Lewis and I took a vote for where we should seek winter quarters, we gave both her—and York—a vote as well. "Perhaps someday this shall be the way of the whole United States," Lewis quipped, but we both knew our country was a long time from anything so forward thinking.

As a result of the vote, we left our miserable camp on the north shore of the bay where we were never completely out of the reach of the tides, yet could find no good ground higher, and where the ocean's waves—once such a source of a joy—roared so incessantly I thought I'd surely go mad with the noise.

We found a location on a bit of high ground on the southern shore, close enough to a small river flowing into the bay that we had fresh water for drinking again, yet remained sheltered by forest. The elk were more plentiful on the southern side of the bay, we had been told, and it seemed to be so. We had also sent a small party south to make salt from seawater, to supply both our present needs and our journey home, and we needed to look in on them. To my surprise, when she learned of it, Janey begged to go along, as she had traveled all this distance and had never before seen the ocean.

One of the curiosities we were determined to see was a blue whale which had beached days before. Of course, by the time we reached it, guided by a young man of the local people, the carcass had been stripped, and all that remained was the skeleton. Still, it was a wonder. Janey's delight in the great ocean and amazement over the bones of the enormous fish were enough to soothe any annoyance I might feel at the constant roll and roar of the waves.

And there was a new marvel—she set little Pomp down to play in the sand and helped him stand. While there, he took his first steps, falling often but squealing with laughter.

I watched them, throat aching—the babe and his mother, who was barely more than a girl herself, catching him up in her arms and romping into the foamy edge of a wave, adding her squeals to Pomp's as she bent to let him trail his fingers in the water. Then she brought him back up the shore and became absorbed in picking through the shells and small stones littering the beach.

It was early January, yet we could all walk about barefoot despite the cold water.

I thought back on our miserable Christmas day celebration. Rancid elk meat, spoiled fish, and some roots. No bread or sweets as we had once known. And I knew not whether Janey knew the significance of the day—the nativity of One meant to be Savior of the world—but she entered into it with a whole heart as well, presenting me most shyly with a bundle that turned out to be twenty-four weasel tails, such as adorned the tippet her people had given Lewis. I marveled over the softly furred bits. Where and how had she gotten them? Did she intend me to attach these to the otter-skin coat I'd obtained at her expense just weeks before? Was this her way of letting me know she did not hold that transaction against me?

Never had I more wished I could speak with her directly. Any attempt to communicate with her met only with thinly veiled hostility from her husband.

Not that I could blame him. She was darling, no matter the people she might have been born of or the circumstances that had brought her here.

I shook myself and turned away, lest Charbonneau catch me staring and I further stir his ire.

Chapter Fourteen

Sacagawea

Three moons we spent there near the sea, or so they said, since we so rarely could see the moon. What a land of rain and mist it was! And yet the warmest winter I had ever known.

It helped somewhat when the houses were completed for us to move in. Our skin lodge was in shreds, so the dry warmth of the log walls seemed a rare luxury by comparison.

Little One learned to walk well and babbled happily. His *ma-ma-ma* warmed my heart, and he ate eagerly of anything I offered, but snuggling for him to take my milk was still my favorite time of the day.

Food remained occasionally scarce, although I was able to forage for roots and the hunters brought in what should have been enough elk and waterfowl. We were at least all able to replenish our store of clothing. Clark quietly continued giving me hides and other goods, and I now had three dresses—one to wear and two for spares. I kept those two rolled up in my pack, ready for whenever we would depart upriver once more.

Preparing even for that was a hardship. We could not afford to wait for the agai to begin their journey upriver, to supply us with food, and I knew Clark and Lewis had traded as many of their pots and kettles as they dared for the beautiful canoes of the Clatsop and Chinook people. Near the end of what they called *March,* we loaded what canoes they could acquire and once again traveled upstream.

This was the hardest season for the peoples who lived along the river as well. We were cold and wet often, so much that even Little One was often fretful. The riverbanks, relatively uninhabited when we had passed through before winter, were now crowded with those expecting the soon-coming swim of the agai. They proved as fretful as Little One, and everyone's patience thinned—even Clark and Lewis, whose actions were uncharacteristically rash time and again.

At last it was decided we could go no further on the river—the water was too high and too fast for safety—and we should go overland to the Chopunnish. But then trying to buy horses—oh! I saw Clark trading his fancy dress coat, and when faced with trying to purchase a horse for Little One and me, my husband took the shirt off of his own back, which I had made of elk skin over the winter, and in a growl asked me for my extra dresses. "Come now, I know you have them," he insisted, and I hastened to pull them from my pack.

A horse, any horse, was better than extra clothing in this moment. And I should be glad I had something to contribute to our journey's needs.

*****

Clark—April-May 1806

The return trip looked like it might be the death of us.

Between the difficulty of the river and the scarcity of food, Lewis and I were not sure how we were to survive. Though knowledge of our concerns passed in glances between us, we never spoke of it out loud. Too much was at stake. But I could see it in Lewis's fraying temper, indeed had already observed it as the winter wore on and Lewis fussed about the inconstancy of the Indian peoples.

I reminded him often that we were here to build relations and establish a basis for trade. He snapped that they had already been ruined by such trade.

Upriver, we began trading for horses, and I took a few men and went off to explore possible river routes into the southwest and even as far as California. While I was gone, Lewis had an altercation with the local people and decided we should rather burn our canoes than let anyone of them benefit from our castoffs.

Our first few days on horseback were attended by many mishaps, amongst which was Charbonneau failing to secure his horses on their picket overnight, resulting in two missing. That took a full day and more to recover them. Then it was our good fortune, led as we were by a Chopunnish man, that we happened upon a Wallahwallah village where a captive Shoshoni woman lived, and through her and Janey we were able to have a long talk with these people.

Then it was off to where the Chopunnish themselves dwelt, to hopefully recover the horses we had left there. On the way, we were once again reduced to eating horses and dogs, the latter of which many of the men stated they came to prefer over horseflesh or even venison or beef, though I never could reconcile myself to the taste. Lewis bragged that he did not mind it, then found himself unaccountably provoked by an Indian host who ridiculed us for our poor eating habits.

Arriving in the region of the Chopunnish, our hopes for a speedy continuation of the journey were dashed by the growing sight of the great mountains all clothed in white. Our Chopunnish hosts confirmed—the high passes were yet deep with snow. They expected we would not find it safe to cross over for at least another moon or more.

Chapter Fifteen

Sacagawea

The Chopunnish provided an unexpectedly pleasant lull in our journey. A young man of the Agai'dika, taken captive like myself, allowed us to speak more fully, although at first he thought himself too good to speak to me. Husband and I enjoyed a small lodge to ourselves, and while the other men may not have been fully content with the wait for the great snows to melt, neither did it seem they suffered overmuch. I could see that the Chopunnish women were friendly, their men amenable to sharing, and—after seeing him resist women's advances in village after village, I am sure I glimpsed Clark slipping away into the dark with a particularly handsome Chopunnish woman.

I smiled to myself. I was happy if he found some comfort, yet it seemed odd to me as well. But why should he not? Nearly all the other men, York included, enjoyed women's attentions in the various places we stayed.

After a moon had passed, we loaded our horses and set out for that beautiful, treacherous path across the highest mountains, only to find it breast-deep with snow. We had to turn back, meaning a longer stay with the Chopunnish.

I busied myself with gathering and drying roots for the journey. Little One took sick, and Clark, Lewis, and the others were much concerned for him. However, with careful treatment, he began to recover. Other members of our party were also ill surrounding that time.

Finally we were able to set out, accompanied by three men of the Chopunnish to guide us. The journey this time was as wearing as before, but we did cross. Clark and Lewis had already planned once they reached the other side of the Great Divide, as they called it, that their party would split three ways. Lewis was to take a group and go farther north to the river they had called Maria's. The rest of us would continue riding down to where we had met my people last summer, find the hidden canoes and supplies, then split again. As we approached the country of my birth, I was able to point out the way, and Clark seemed well pleased by my guidance. It gave me no small measure of pride to be able to do this service.

At Three Forks, having found our canoes and stores, Clark sent Ordway and others downstream. Then, taking myself, Little One, my husband, and eight other men, we rode across country to find the southernmost river.

Upon reaching the river called the Yellowstone, Clark split the group again. Husband and I stayed with him. Two dugout canoes were made and furnished, and we found ourselves floating downriver most pleasantly. Many an hour I spent entertaining Little One by pointing out various birds and creatures and gazing with my own wonder upon the high rocky bluffs that gave this stream its name.

One notable formation Clark called "Pompey's Pillar" after his name for my boy. There was much affection in his eyes and voice for the child, more than even my husband showed.

The other small group of men who Clark had charged to take our horses overland to the towns of the Minnetaree caught up with us shortly, outfitted in small craft made of buffalo skin and without their horses, which they said had been stolen by a neighboring people. Clark brushed it off, and we kept traveling. Before many days we met up with Lewis and the others—but Lewis had a bad wound in his hinder parts. Clark dressed it, and Lewis lay in one of the canoes as we traveled, seeking to recover.

It was, I thought, as close as I had ever seen him to dying.

Husband told me that Lewis and a handful of others had gotten into a gunfight with warriors who lived to the north and had traded with the French and British for firearms. Lewis was shot in the backside, and though the ball went through, he suffered much from the wound, having to ride on horseback until they met up with the rest of the men in canoes.

Faster than I thought possible, we arrived back in the lands where I had been taken as a child—the towns of the Minnetaree and Mandan. Had those fierce people kept their word to no longer make war on the Agai'dika? We soon heard that the Sioux, to the south, had continued making war on the Minnetaree despite their promises to Lewis and Clark to not do so. I had little hope that the Agai'dika were safe either.

But here we were, and while Clark and Lewis prepared to finish their journey downriver, it was determined that they no longer needed my husband's services as interpreter, since the great chief Black Cat of the Mandan declined to travel with them for fear of the Sioux. And so my husband received his payment and was offered to come along without pay, but he declined. This was where he could best make a living, he told Clark.

I did not know how to feel that the journey was over for me. Part of me had looked forward to seeing the towns of the white men, but I feared it as well. Yet I had gone with them all the way west to what some peoples called the Stinking Lake, with its never-ending waves, and back again. What would one more adventure have been?

The sun glinted red off of the strands of Clark's hair and beard as he looked long at Little One, then at me, and finally turned back to my husband before speaking quietly. Husband took a long breath and turned to me. "He wishes to take our son and raise him as his own."

A pang struck my heart. Was I to be deprived of my son as well as the people of my birth? As I considered, Clark spoke again, more urgently, and my husband went on, "He says our son will enjoy every advantage he can give him in the society of the white man."

My eyes stung. "He is still too young," I protested.

Husband conveyed those words to him, or so I presumed. Clark spoke again.

"He asks, when the boy is old enough to leave his mother, will we consider such a thing?"

I realized then—the world was changing. These white men had traveled to the far west and back and arrived safely. Would anything be beyond their reach before long?

Who knew what adventures my Little One might enjoy in his lifetime?

I found myself nodding slowly, despite the burn in my throat and the ache in my chest. "When he is old enough to leave his mother, then we will consider it."

As my husband translated, Clark met my gaze with a warm smile. He nodded and thanked me—thanked us, Charbonneau said—but the warmth eased the pain in my heart and filled me to my toes and fingers.

I may not ever have had a choice in coming to this place, to being wife to this man, to accompanying these explorers on this journey, but who knew how Creator might use it. Might use my son.

Might yet use me.

In that moment, I was glad.

The End

Is that it? What happened after? How much of this is fictional?

Those are the sorts of questions I've been asked with this story. It's admittedly different from anything I've written before. As I drew heavily from the Lewis and Clark journals, it seemed natural to structure this story as if it were Sacagawea's own telling.

And how much of it was true? The actual events I've covered, certainly. I've embellished some detail, but the main events are as reported in the journals. There was no indication that Lewis was actually present for Sacagawea's labor, but given his intense curiosity about anything scientific, including medical and cultural details, it wouldn't be a stretch for him to have popped in at some point to observe. He comments in his journal on the difference he had marked in ease of an Indian woman's labor depending upon whether the father is white or Indian—very interesting, but I'm sure attributable to other factors. Yet the fact remains that this is evidence of his interest in such things. Clark's relationship with a Chopunnish (Nez Perce) woman is also a matter of speculation and/or legend, with a Nez Perce warrior claiming years later to be his son. Most of the men on the expedition did, indeed, accept favors from the Native women as often as I mention in the story, possibly more. Lewis also mulls in his journal the question of whether venereal diseases were universal to all peoples or whether they were spread from the Europeans to indigenous Americans.

As always, I found a wealth of information I could not include in a mere novella. Yes, William Clark did wind up adopting Sacagawea's son, Jean Baptiste Charbonneau. An adoption is also recorded for a daughter, Lizette Charbonneau, but she is never again mentioned in historical documents, so it's presumed she died in infancy. Sacagawea herself is recorded as having died of "putrid fever" in 1812, at Fort Lisa, South Dakota (some sources say North Dakota). Oral tradition states that she survived but left Charbonneau and returned to the west, where she lived to old age. The Hidatsa have their own traditions surrounding her. All that is covered on Wikipedia, which provides a very useful introduction and overview of her life.

Perhaps the most pressing question is, how does a story about Sacagawea (or Sacajawea, more about that in a moment) wind up in the middle of a collection focused on human trafficking?

Many do not know she was the survivor of slavery, twice over—once when taken by the Minnetarees (Hidatsa) from the Shoshone people at age 11, and once again when she was given to Toussaint Charbonneau as wife, probably at age 13 or 14. That would have made her about 16 during the Lewis and Clark expedition—or as young as 14. Lewis states that she had been taken five years before their encounter with the Shoshone, while another expedition member states three.

Regardless of age, she has become a symbol of courage and tenacity, and for good reason. Though traditionally credited as a guide for the Lewis and Clark expedition, which was not strictly accurate, in truth her contribution was much wider. She served as both interpreter and guide, but also supported the endeavor in quiet ways such as foraging for food and eventually serving as a symbol of peace and good will in situations where strange men traveling alone were viewed with suspicion. All of this, of course, was accomplished while caring for her own baby.

So is it "Sacagawea" or "Sacajawea"? I admit to a bit of bias, having lived in North Dakota for the past decade and more, where we have a Lake Sakakawea. After careful study of the debate behind the different spellings and pronunciations, I chose to go with what Lewis and Clark recorded in their own journals. Whether you pronounce that with a hard G (as in *gate)* or a soft one (as in *giraffe)* is, I suppose, up to you, but they also record the meaning of her name as "Bird Woman," which as the Hidatsa name comes with a "k" and not a "j" sound. (All that is more fully explained on Wikipedia.)

I drew inspiration for the title from Scott O'Dell's novel *Streams to the River, River to the Sea.* I nearly used the fictional name *Naya Nuki* for Sacagawea's friend from the novel by Kenneth Thomasma, until I happened upon her true name, *Poppank* or Jumping Fish, as recorded in the unabridged Lewis and Clark journals. It is also known that Native peoples often changed their names depending upon their stage of life or accomplishments.

For those expecting a more "Christian" story—well, I wasn't really able to produce that this time. I write from my own worldview as a believer in Christ, but honesty compels me as always to portray people as they thought and behaved in the context of their own time. I find it doubtful that Lewis professed Christianity at all, while Clark's faith seems very nominal. Sacagawea herself would have had consciousness of a Creator and the spiritual nature of the world around her. I hope the reader will find the story redemptive, and a reminder that even where men do not necessarily acknowledge Him, God is still very often at work. I found myself astonished at how this expedition met peril after peril and yet only lost one member early on.

Overall, I have tried to keep my focus on Sacagawea's thoughts and feelings rather than the minutiae of the journey itself. I've made what I hope are educated guesses on her attitude toward being taken from her original people and then her marriage to Charbonneau. Though some have regarded slavery as a problem confined to the American South, perpetrated only against Blacks of African descent by whites of European descent, in reality, the issue of trafficking in human lives and bodies, whether for labor or prostitution, is endemic to human history, across millennia and cultures. Native American peoples practiced it extensively, and the Shoshone were not the only ones to be impoverished by oppression from other indigenous nations. It is a question, of course, whether in their travels Lewis and Clark honestly wished to better the situation of the Shoshone and others, or whether they only sought economic gain and so used the Native peoples to that end. Both were, however, products of their own upbringing as well.

Clark did seem to hold genuine affection for Sacagawea and her son (and no, there is no mention anywhere of a romantic relationship with her), while seeing no contradiction in his desire to raise that child as his own, or in his later refusal to free York, who also gave invaluable service to the expedition.

I realized too late that I should probably have featured York's viewpoint in this story instead of Clark's—or perhaps written a different story altogether. While on deadline for this one, I had the honor of meeting a young man who is the survivor of a modern forced-labor scam, and who now works with an excellent organization that fights all forms of human trafficking. I wished that I'd had time to talk to him and develop something on this aspect of the contemporary problem of slavery. This was, however, what most convinced me I needed to press on with writing Sacagawea's story. Even though she never found "rescue" in the most obvious sense, her voice deserves to be heard.

I hope I have honored her well.

ACKNOWLEDGEMENTS

My deepest thanks to all those who helped me on this particular journey.

Ken Thomasma, for his little volume, *The Truth About Sacajawea*.

Suzy Avey of the Sacajawea Interpretive Center in Salmon, Idaho, for specially opening the center and answering my questions, before the start of their official season.

Beth Goddard and Lee S. King, always lending a sympathetic ear, an encouraging word, and more prayers than I'm sure I know about.

Michelle Griep, for the best critiques ever.

Devin Joubert, for your very enthusiastic pre-read.

Brian Lawrence and Angela Shelton, for honoring me as your co-author on this volume and for very helpful thoughts and feedback as well.

Sarah Hanks, for helming Brave Authors (and encouraging me to stay onboard).

Sarah Everest, for ninja editorial skills.

My youngest daughter Meeghan, for always being up for a road trip—and whose real-life dilemma of returning a car became the means of my getting to actually see more of the Lewis and Clark Trail.

My middle daughters Breanna and Corrie, for encouragement, support, and an always-willing read.

My oldest daughter Erin, for faithfully bringing the grandboys over and reminding me why I do this—but also for letting me have that one weekend to focus on finishing (even though I missed them terribly!!).

My sons—who to my amazement are all now fathers, and doing a marvelous job of it—and their beautiful wives and children, for further reminders of why I do this.

The members of our new congregation at Trinity Free Lutheran, for your encouragement and prayers during this crazy past year.

My husband Troy—always. That is all.

My Lord and Savior, Creator of all worlds known and unknown . . . once more, You've called me out into the wildness of what I thought I could not do, and here it is, a written story. Wow. Just . . . wow.

Unbroken

Angela D. Shelton

Chapter 1

Team Hero

"Go, Nova!" Mrs. Well's voice roars over the thunder of the crowd cheering me on. "Nice serve. Do it again."

I swipe at the sweat beading on my forehead. With a record-breaking number of spectators packed in the senior high gym, the temperature broils. Hard to believe I can hear Jenny's mom through the echo chamber of chanting fans. She seldom misses an event and does her best to root for me almost as much as she does her own daughter.

We've got to win this one to slide into the ideal bracket in the finals. No pressure, but my best friend, Jenny, stares at me with pleading eyes. As if I need the reminder. It's the game point serve, and I could end this now if I hit it right. Who knows? If I cinch it, maybe coach will consider me for the team captain next year. Wouldn't that make the most amazing senior year ever?

Deep breath in—exhale slow. *You've got this. You're a pro.*

A girl in our opponent's back row shifts her weight, eyes wide, feet unsure.

Perfect. She's mine.

Tossing the ball high, I rise like lightning, and unleash the Nova Slammer straight at her dark, curly tresses.

The volleyball torpedoes in her direction, and her legs panic. Instead of getting underneath it, as the angle required, she steps back, her frame unlocked and weak. The orb slams into her left arm and spirals into the stands.

Our team erupts into screams of delight with the scoreboard declaring our win to the applauding crowd. Jenny rushes me forward with the rest of our squad, and we dance in place like we've joined a mosh pit at a heavy metal concert. Some chant my name. "Nova. Nova. Nova." I'm lighter than an overfilled balloon.

Coach Jones joins us for a moment of celebration, then pulls back. "Let's not forget to thank our opponents, ladies."

We line up and file past the other team, slapping hands one-by-one. The girl I'd targeted shuffles along at the end of the human train, focusing on the heels of the player in front of her. It doesn't take a rocket scientist to know how she's hurting. Like she's failed her teammates, her friends.

It's my turn to tap her raised palm. Instead, I put a hand on her arm. The move garners her attention, and our eyes meet. I've been in her shoes before, feeling like the weak link. If only I could encourage her. "Good match. You almost had us a few times there."

Pink washes her cheeks. Anger? Embarrassment? "Yeah, right."

She brushes my hand away and stalks off to the locker room.

Sore loser.

Whatever.

We head to the showers, floating on air and excited about our celebration party. Coach buys pizza when we win, and tonight, we feast at Slice of Heaven, our favorite hangout. It's good to be the hero for the night.

Chapter 2

The One

"I don't think I can eat another bite." My plate shows the crust evidence of the three slices of supreme pizza I've devoured, and I rub my belly for effect. "Unless there's dessert."

Jenny laughs and pokes my shoulder. "That's what you said after the second slice."

It's hard to contain my grin when I take in her freckled face. "You've got something right here." I point at my chin to show her where she's missed a gob of sauce.

She swipes at the goop with a napkin but her gaze trails beyond me and her eyes widen. "Nova, behind you. Heartbreak alert."

When I turn, I instantly understand her distraction. A group of guys follow a waitress to a nearby table, and one of them could model for Levi's or some overpriced cologne. Dark wavy hair lies longer over his forehead than the sides, giving him a sultry vibe. He's at least six feet tall. It's so unfair for a guy to have such long eyelashes, but they complement his sun-kissed skin.

He drapes his leather jacket over the back of his chair and shows the attendant a 100-watt smile the moment she hands him a menu.

The waitress seems as spellbound as I feel. She giggles and twirls a lock of her mane around her finger without writing a word he's saying. For her sake, I hope she's got a memory like a safe, but I doubt she'll remember a thing about what he orders.

I think I'm in love, but I'm also a realist. "He's out of our league, and a lot older too. I'll bet he's at least a senior in college."

A dreamy smile tugs at Jenny's lips. She props her elbow on the table and rests her chin in her hand, eyes fixed on him. "You never know. Could be he's into younger women."

We've been besties since kindergarten, and Jenny's heart trips over every handsome face she encounters. "You're pitiful, you know that?"

Because she doesn't respond, I give her a playful cuff on the back of her head, jolting her back to reality.

She glares. "Hey. A girl can dream."

Kenny Jones, the most awkward and gangly teen in our entire class, hovers over a pinball machine in the corner, off the main dining room. I point. "That's the kid we get to dream about. Our age and speed."

Her eye roll is classic Jenny. "We've got prom to prepare for. Who would you rather have walk you in, Kenny . . ." She eyes our classmate, who smacks the apparatus with his palm—a sure sign he's lost his last ball. She turns toward the other guy and sighs. "Or Mr. Dreamy Eyes?"

If only she didn't have such a significant argument. "I assure you, our chances of showing up with Kenny are one hundred times better than our odds with Mr. Eyes."

She shrugs. "Come on. I'll beat you in air hockey."

"Fat chance."

Chapter 3

No Way!

The puck slams into the slot on Jenny's side, and I raise my fist in triumph. "And that's a wrap. Two out of three means the Nova Slammer reigns victorious once more."

I take an exaggerated bow, as if we have an audience enthralled with our competition.

Jenny holds up two quarters. "Three out of five?"

Never able to deny my best friend another opportunity to get slaughtered, I nod. "You're on."

She sets the coins on the edge of the table. "Give me a minute to run to the ladies' room. Won't be long."

Since I'd watched Jenny down enough Gatorade during the tournament to float a navy and then the additional four sodas at dinner, I know her eyeballs are swimming right now. "I'll set it up."

The quarters slip easily into the machine, and it hums to life. The puck clatters into the dispenser, primed for our first round. A ball from the miniature basketball game bounces my way. I grab the escapee, ready to hand it back to whoever chases it. Mr. Eyes turns from his friends and gives me a slow grin. My mouth goes dry.

I hold the orb out to him, and a tingle runs up my arm. Are my lips forming a smile? They're too numb to tell.

A glint flickers in his eyes, his perfect teeth glowing. How had I missed that square jaw and five o'clock shadow?

He accepts it from me and winks. "I couldn't help but notice you and your team are celebrating tonight. I'll bet you're the captain of the squad, aren't you?"

Is it really possible that he noticed *me*? My jaw clenches so taut it aches. "That would be Jenny, my best friend. She's in the ladies' room."

Did I just tell Mr. Eyes—Mr. Literal Perfection—that Jenny went to the ladies' room? Idiot move.

His eyes gleam with something unreadable that sets my heart pounding in my chest. "Well, I'm certain you're her star player. I'm new to the area. This your favorite haunt?"

Where am I again? I allow my gaze to trail around the room. Slice of Heaven. Our favorite hang-out. *Yes.* Say it out loud, you dolt. "Yes. We love this place. Good pizza." *Good pizza?* Has my brain gone on vacation?

He nods, and a curl dips below his eyebrow. He sweeps it back with the rest of his gorgeous locks. "I'm Damian."

"Nova."

"Beautiful name for a beautiful woman."

No one ever called me beautiful—or a woman, for that matter. My tongue is drier than the Sahara. "Thank you."

"Perhaps we could go out sometime? I can give you my number."

Heat rushes to my cheeks. Did he just . . . *me* . . . he wants to go out with me? "My phone's at the table." Who cares where your phone is? "I'll share mine."

He slips his cell out of his back pocket and taps in the digits I recite. "There. I sent you a text."

A tap on my shoulder turns my attention to Jenny, back from the ladies' room. She waggles her eyebrows at me, acting like a ten-year-old. Ready to tease.

If I could scream, I would. I send her a silent message with my glare. *Please don't embarrass me in front of Damian.*

She stares past me to him. "I'm Jenny, Nova's best friend."

Her title sounds so juvenile. Do college guys have besties?

Damian nods at her but moves his focus back to me. "I need to head back to my friends. Text me?"

Though I nod, I'm fairly confident my smile makes me look like a love-sick kid. "Yeah. Sure."

It's gotten late by the time I climb the steps to the apartment I share with my mother. Near the top, the soft flicker of the television spills through the living room window, casting light across our small porch. Mom's home. I hesitate. Should I tell her about Damian? If I keep it to myself, she can't warn me off or worry about him being older. We used to talk about everything, but lately . . . it's easier to hold some things private. This is too personal. Too complicated. And honestly, I'm not sure I want her opinion tonight.

Digging my key out of my book bag, I open the door, flipping the lock on the double bolt like I've done hundreds of times. We don't really do curfews anymore since my life revolves around the sport of the season. As long as I check in every couple of hours until bedtime, she trusts me to handle myself.

Rounding the corner into the living room, I find her curled up on the couch snoring, the laugh track from a late-night comedy bouncing off the walls. She must've conked out a while ago because she only puts that show on when she's too tired to think.

Unsure how to wake her without causing a heart attack, I pause.

"Mom, I'm home," I whisper.

Nothing.

I try again, louder this time. Still no response.

With a sigh, I cross the room and touch her shoulder. "I'm home."

She jolts upright, clutching her chest like I dropped out of the ceiling in a ski mask. "Nova, you scared me."

Every time.

With a grimace, I drop my book bag at my feet. "Sorry, I tried not to."

The tired smile she gives me cramps my heart. If my dad cared even a little, he'd stop dodging work each time the court garnished his wages. Instead, he slips away, job to job, while Mom trades time with me for long nights at work.

With a loud yawn, she pushes off the couch and stretches, her joints popping. "How'd your night go? Did you win?"

"Yes, I think we've got a real shot at state this year."

Her face lights up, and she pulls me into a warm hug. "I'm so proud of you. You know that, right?"

I nod into her shoulder. I do know, but I hate that she needs to run herself ragged to keep us afloat. If I could help more—if he helped at all—maybe she wouldn't be so wiped out every night. If she could come to a single one of my games. Just once, I'd love to see her in the bleachers, cheering for me like Mrs. Wells does. Someday.

Until then, wouldn't it be amazing if Damian showed up to cheer one day? Someone for me alone. A girl can dream.

A buzz alerts me to another message from him. Perhaps the dream is closer than I think.

Chapter 4

Secret

"He's too old for you." Jenny glares at me via my tablet screen. She's wearing her fuzzy pink PJs, and she's propped up against her headboard for our nightly chat session while I cuddle into my favorite purple pillow, Super Fluff. "Your mom will never allow you to go out with him."

It's been a week of back-and-forth texts all hours of the day and night with Damian. Getting to know each other. Sharing our latest ambitions. But he hasn't asked me on a date yet, a fact that irritates me now that Jenny's brought it up.

"Who said anything about going out?" I glance over at my phone, struggling to contain my desire to scoop it up and look for Damian's response to my last text. "We're simply talking."

"But he will, you know it. Then what will you do?"

"Look. It's late, and if we don't cut this off soon, Mom's going to hear me. I don't want my electronics banned again." Our argument takes us five minutes past my deadline for calls on school nights. It would be bad enough to lose my evening connection to Jenny, but losing phone privileges would cost me my link to Damian as well. "I'll see you in the morning."

"Fine." She grabs her pillow from behind her head and punches it into shape. "But this discussion isn't over."

"Fine." I stab the red button to hang up. "But it's over for now."

Now that I'm alone, I scroll through our messages, eager to re-read what he's written so far, in case I missed some subtle nuance in our conversation.

Damian: UR so easy 2 talk 2.

Me: Easier than UR college friends?

Damian: UR more mature than a lot of women.

He thinks I'm mature. Jenny doesn't understand.

Me: U never said. What year are u in?

Please let him be a freshman or a sophomore. Anything but a senior.

Damian: Still don't have the senior swagger. U?

Me: Not yet. Soon though.

Is a year and a half soon? Close enough.

Damian: Nice. I'd love U to join me at State.

Eeps. He wants me to go to his school. I can almost picture it. The two of us walking hand-in-hand to classes every day.

At an abrupt knock, I shove the phone under the covers. Mom opens the door and pokes her head in. "Congratulations on another win. I wish I could have been there."

Anguish fills her eyes the way it does when she misses a life event because she's working late. Time for the reassurance dance we play on repeat. "It's okay. I know you were there in spirit."

She gives me her familiar sad smile, sits on the edge of my bed, and tucks a strand of hair behind my ear. "You know I'd be there if I could."

Yes. I've known this for years. If we still lived as a family of three instead of the two of us. But that isn't our life. "I know you would have."

"Anything new and exciting besides your win?"

She asks this every chance she gets. Whenever she arrives home early enough for us to eat supper together, it's the most important topic of discussion. I always prattle off the goings on at school or something that happened with Jenny. But I'm not ready to share about Damian. It's still too personal. Too private. More now that we've been learning everything about each other. It's like I really know him, deep down.

I stifle a yawn and hedge. "The win felt pretty huge."

"Well, you need to get some rest." She tucks the blanket under my chin like I'm five years old again. "I love you, baby girl. Sleep well."

"And don't let the bedbugs bite."

With a peck on my forehead, she flicks off the light and closes the door behind her. Guilt squirms in my belly like a dark creature preparing a nest. I'll tell her about him—eventually.

Chapter 5

Attention

We aren't supposed to have our phones out during classes. The minute hand on the clock above Mr. Yoman's head creeps forward, and I'm convinced my laser-focus must have broken it. U.S. History has never been duller than today. It's not the subject, per se, but his monotone voice droning on and on, ticking facts off.

The desire to sneak a peek at my cell is almost unbearable. I haven't texted Damian all day, not wanting to look desperate, but I still check my phone too often.

Jenny's glazed expression tells me she's just as bored as I am.

The bell chimes, providing blessed relief from the lecture, but Mr. Yoman hollers to be heard above the shuffle of movement. "Read chapter twelve and answer the questions at the end for tomorrow's class. There may be a pop quiz." It's his constant threat, though we've only had one so far this semester.

I scurry out the door, following the flow of traffic while I dig my phone out of my backpack. My heart leaps into my throat. There's a text from Damian.

Damian: Are U thinking of me? Because I can't stop thinking about U.

How to respond without sounding like a desperate child?

Me: I am. How's your day been?

There. I like it. Casual, friendly, and not at all desperate.

Damian: Lonely. Classes have dragged today. U busy tonight?

Me: I've got a game.

Damian: Oh. :(

In the hallway shuffle, something smacks my hand, and my phone drops to the hallway floor. I reach for it, but someone kicks it away, and it skitters through the crowd of students. The bell chimes again. I scramble and recapture it, rush to my next class.

I didn't have time to respond before the tardy alarm. That gnaws at me for the entire forty-five minutes. Our AP English Language teacher, Ms. Freeman, confiscates any electronic device she finds, so I don't dare sneak it out. She's going into minute detail—will her lecture ever end? It's the last one for today, then I'm free to text Damian as much as I'd like until the varsity team plays.

The room erupts into motion with the ending chime, and I dig my phone out without bothering to get out of my chair.

He'd gone silent after his previous message, no doubt waiting for my idiotic self to respond. What would a mature college woman say?

Me: Available this weekend.

What possessed me to offer that? I haven't told Mom about him, much less disclosed his age. Possibly she wouldn't stress over a few years' difference. I'll have to broach the subject with caution.

Mom hasn't been on a date since my father left us. She insists it's best for her to remain single and not bring another man into our home. I think she's afraid. But just because she's out of the dating world doesn't mean I'm going to stay unmarried for my entire life. It's my choice, not hers.

But I know the issue isn't whether I'll date or marry someday. The issue is that I'm seventeen. Still underage. And he's in college.

We dress for the game. I check my phone. Nothing.

We do our warmups. I check my phone. Nothing.

We plant ourselves in the bleachers, ready to cheer on the JV team. I look at my screen every few minutes. Nothing. Nothing. Nothing.

Rejection propels my heart further toward my stomach each time I sneak a peek at my cell. If I don't quit looking, my battery will die before the night's out. I slide it beneath my thigh, determined not to look again until the JV match is over.

A buzz rumbles, and my heart gallops. A message.

Mom: Good luck tonight, baby girl. I know you'll do great!

She puts enough ribbons and trophies after her sentences to make it look like we've won the state championship. Like that matters right now.

Me: TY

I cram the stupid device back under my leg.

An elbow digs into my ribs. Jenny's lips are twisted as if someone stuck week-old gym socks up her nose. She points toward the entrance. "You expecting a guest?"

And then I hear it. My name shouted over the din of the room. Damian waves from the open double doors. His handsome grin glowing just for me.

Chapter 6

Taking Control

"I can't believe you came." Unable to stop smiling, I must look like I'm crushing. I don't recall telling him what school I went to. When I first got my phone, Mom laid down the law: never share my personal information with anyone she hasn't met. "How did you know where we played?"

He's more gorgeous than the first time I saw him. Hair slicked back, still damp from a shower, he's got a spicy scent that sends my heart into palpitations, and his dark, stubbled chin holds the cutest dimple. "You wore your uniform, remember?"

I glance back at the bleachers at my team, where I'm supposed to be sitting, cheering on the JV squad. Jenny stares at us, her lips flattened into her no-nonsense grimace.

He presses a kiss to the top of my head, sending my pulse into spasms. "It doesn't take much research to find out which local school is the Mighty Tiger's home."

Of course, it would be easy to figure out, but he'd made the effort. Heat rushes to my cheeks. "It's not college-level yet, but I'm hoping for a scholarship."

"Looks like your friend isn't happy to see me." He points toward Jenny, who's now glaring at us, arms crossed. "I can leave if you're uncomfortable."

"Ignore her." *Because I'm sure going to.* "I need to head back to the bench, though. Coach will have my hide if I miss too much of the JV's match. Will you stay until after I play?"

He winks, sending a shiver down my arm. "That's why I came, silly."

If I were capable, I'm certain I would float all the way back to join my team. Eventually, I take the floor beside them, stealing glances his way too often. Here, with every beautiful girl in the entire school surrounding me—even the cheer team in their tiny skirts—I only ever see his eyes on me. *Me*.

Spurred on by his attention, I nail my serves. The squad and I are on fire, and the opposing players are paying the price, getting more flustered with each point we score. The Tigers are unbeatable, and my heart soars the moment the winning volley goes our way.

I can't tell if the excitement vibrating through my body is from the win or my main fan. It's the first time in forever someone's in the stands just for me.

We line up and thank the visiting team before we head to the showers. It's tough to stick with my teammates while Damian moves toward the door. I want to run after him and beg him to wait, but Coach insists on a post-game debriefing, no excuses.

Blah, blah, blah. I ignore most of Coach Jones's too-long speech. We won. Can't we be happy and move on? When she releases us, I'm tempted to rush to see if Damian waited. But I know I'm ripe, and that's not how I want him to see me—or smell me.

Jenny and I rarely bathe after games since our ancient school still runs communal showers. I don't hesitate though and dash into the water before it's hot. Jenny follows, clothes still on, and leans against a wall, out of the water's reach. "I don't like him. He's too old for you, Nova."

This again. "I'll be in college in a year and a half. You wouldn't say he's too old for me then, would you?"

"By the time you enroll, he's going to have graduated. Do you know how old he is? He sure doesn't look young enough to be a junior to me." I rush back to my locker, towel clutched around me, with her trailing behind. "And why is he so interested in a high school girl? Have you asked yourself that?"

The sting of her words strikes like the lash of a whip. "You mean he couldn't be interested in *me*—right? Because I'm not pretty enough?"

Her frown deepens. "I didn't say that. I've never said . . ." She huffs out a breath, and her gaze turns pleading. "You're beautiful, and smart, and the most amazing friend ever. I'm worried about you. You're obsessed."

Heat swirls in my gut, and I yank my socks up with such ferocity my finger tears a hole in the thin fabric. No matter. I jam my shoe over it, not bothering to untie and retie the laces.

"You don't understand. Your life is perfect. Two parents to support you and each other, and both have decent jobs. Money is never a problem for your family. Your father even comes to our games with your mom."

Her ears redden, a sure sign I've ticked her off. "So, it's my fault your dad took off?"

Metal clangs as the locker door rattles from the slam, pain shooting through my elbow where it connects. Silence ripples through the room before voices tentatively rise again. With eyes burning into my back, I lean closer and murmur, "Let me have this one opportunity to be special to someone."

Moisture rims her eyes. "You've always been special to me."

She doesn't understand. No one does. "I gotta go."

With a quick swipe across her cheek, she erases a tear. "Wait. We're your ride home."

"I can walk."

"Nova, don't. Wait."

But I ignore her. I'm tired of being the pitiful case who catches rides with friends because her parents are never at the games. Tonight's my chance to take control of my life for once, and I'm not going to miss it.

Chapter 7

The Prince

I can hardly believe it—Damian's waiting for me by the door. He leans against the wall like he owns the place, one foot propped up, hands tucked into his jeans' pockets. If I didn't know better, I'd think I'd wandered onto the set of a hair product commercial. Everything about him appears effortless, cool, perfect.

How could someone like him be interested in me?

Our eyes lock, and he flashes me a slow grin that shoots a tingle skimming up my arms. My mouth goes dry, but I manage a faint, "Hey."

He meets me halfway and slides my book bag off my shoulder. "Let me carry that. You heading for pizza again tonight? The team's gotta celebrate." He presses a hand to the small of my back, warm and inviting. "And you—you played like a star out there."

Heat creeps into my cheeks. He thinks I'm good. "I'm not feeling like a crowd."

"Won't you miss time with your friends?"

"We eat out after every win, and we're closing in on the state championship. We'll have more opportunities." That came out wrong. "I'm not bragging. It's just . . ."

My tongue seems to have a mind of its own. I clamp my lips closed and force it into silence.

Damian brushes a cool finger across my warm cheek. His smile dances in his emerald eyes. "Your team will cinch State. Especially with you on the squad."

The flush of heat travels from my face all the way to my toes. He sees me—not my team. "I hope so."

He gestures toward the doors where the last of the crowd trickles out. "How about a burger instead? My treat."

It's tax season, so Mom will be home late, and she knows I usually have dinner with the team or Jenny and her family. I've got time. "That would be great."

At the far side of the parking lot, a shiny, black Cadillac Escalade with blacked-out windows waits—distant from other vehicles. Darkness looms around it since the lights from the main area don't shine this far out. I'm glad to have him with me. "Nice car."

My comment draws a shrug from him. "My father's money, though I don't mind spending it."

He opens the passenger door and offers me his hand. It's like something out of a fairy tale—the kind where the prince first notices the secret princess, who's been there all along, waiting to be seen. After I'm seated, he shuts the door and tosses my bag into the back seat. The scent of sweat and sneakers clashes with the rich aroma of expensive leather. Handsome and clearly well-off. What are the odds? Am I Cinderella? I want to believe it could be real—just this once.

Chapter 8

All That Glitters

White linen tablecloths and fresh flower centerpieces are not what I'd imagined when Damian invited me for a burger and fries. At least he scores us a table on the back patio where my jeans and pullover are less conspicuous.

A waiter in a black button-down and pants brings us water and takes our orders. I'm grateful they feature a hamburger on the menu in addition to the fancy steaks, seafood, and pastas. Though I've never eaten French fries made with truffle oil and parmesan cheese, how bad can they be?

The server asks to see Damian's ID when he requests wine with his meal. *No way.* With a quick read of his driver's license, the fellow turns his attention to me, and I rush through my request, still processing the fact that Damian is at least twenty-one. I struggle to decide whether this new information makes me feel flattered or creeped out.

Somehow, ordering calms my nervous stomach. If he's used to places like this, I can't believe he stepped into Slice of Heaven, where we first met. Why is he interested in someone like me when he owns a life like this?

Damian clears his throat. "Are you all right?"

What had I missed? "Sure. Why?"

He leans back in his chair and grins, his dazzling smile capturing my attention. "You seem a little uneasy. I don't think your leg's stopped bobbing since we sat down."

I cross my legs and force them to still. "Sorry. I'm a little new at this. It's actually my first date . . . I mean, if this is a date . . ." There goes my tongue again, running wild like a five-year-old in a candy store with a dollar in her fist.

He reaches across the table and places his hand over mine. "I've never met someone so easy to talk to. I can be myself around you."

The waiter returns, balancing a bottle of wine and a soda on a small tray. He sets my drink down first. The ice clinks against the sides, a cool contrast to the warmth rising in my face. He uncorks and pours a stream of dark red into Damian's goblet.

The liquid swirls, rich and elegant, and suddenly our age gap grows more obvious. Damian doesn't belong in my world of high school cafeterias and energy drinks.

Damian lifts his glass, the rim catching the light. "To new relationships."

I raise mine, its icy surface slick on my fingers, and tap it to his. Our glasses meet with a soft chime—his refined, mine simple—and we both take a sip.

My stomach begins its protest anew. Jenny may have had a point. "I'll be right back."

Once I've asked directions, I find the ladies' room, rush into the end stall, and latch the door behind me. My racing heart thunders in my ears, and I lean my forehead against the cool tile wall, gulping in air. It's been years since my last panic attack, so of course, I'm going to have one tonight.

Several deep breaths later, my pulse calms, and the room stops spinning around me. I sniff. Even the bathrooms here smell amazing, like I've stepped into an upscale floral shop instead of a lavatory.

A weight sinks into my torso. Who am I kidding? This place is all wrong. I don't belong here. I don't belong with him. Jenny's right. He's out of my league. We're not in the same universe.

Better to end this now, before someone gets hurt—like me.

I wash my hands with expensive smelling soap. The towels, though disposable, are thick and elegant to my touch. The girl looking back at me from the mirror belongs at a burger joint. They should have stopped me at the entrance.

Uneasy, I return to our table. Damian's glass is half empty, but my own is full once more. Steam drifts up from a bun with a fancy wooden skewer. The fries stand tall, stacked vertically in a silver cone beside the plate. I can't imagine they have ketchup here.

Damian munches on a fry from his own service. "I hate to keep asking, but are you all right? You look a little pale."

"Probably just hungry. The food smells amazing."

I take a bite out of the sandwich. The smoky-buttery flavors dance on my taste buds, and it practically melts in my mouth. The soda chases it down. Next, I nibble a French fry. This, too, is like nothing I've ever experienced. Instead of salty and greasy, it's crisp and nutty. It all tastes like money.

Might as well enjoy this one meal. I doubt I'll see the inside of a place like this again for a long while.

A few minutes of indulgence pass, and my glass is half empty again. Damian signals for the waiter to refill it, then returns his attention to me. "How's your dinner?"

My thoughts slow, like a remote control paused them. "Good." I look around the restaurant and realize how far away the other patrons look.

My arms grow heavy, probably tired from the day's exertion, but it's such an odd sensation.

The server refills my drink, and Damian pushes the goblet toward me. "You're still pale. I think you should sip some more. You may be dehydrated."

Perhaps he's got a point. Is it getting warmer? A wave of heat washes over my body. I down a few more gulps, the slick surface cools my palm. The urge to close my eyes overwhelms me. Something's not right. "Don't . . ." My lips won't cooperate. "feel . . ."

No. I try to stand. The world tilts on its axis, and the table blurs in front of me.

Arms draw me close. Damian's arms. He's got me, holding me firm against him. "I thought something was up. Let's get you out of here."

Cotton fills my mouth, my tongue thick with it. "Want . . . home."

The waiter rushes over, though he walks crooked, like I'm watching him through mirrors in a funhouse. "Is the lady well? Do you need an ambulance?"

Damian crushes me closer to him. "My sister's fine, but she might have sneaked a nip when I wasn't looking. Kids, right? Mom's gonna go nuclear on her."

No. Not sister. I shake my head, but it serves only to make the room spin.

We're shuffling to the door, he's dragging me along. Why doesn't someone help?

"Sir," the server calls from behind us.

Please. Let him see this is wrong. But Damian doesn't slow, and we're out the back door and headed toward his SUV.

The waiter jogs up. "Sorry, but the young lady left her phone on the table."

My phone. I gather my strength and reach for it, but he's too quick, and he snatches it from the guy. "Thanks. She's so forgetful sometimes."

"I hope she's better soon and doesn't land in too much trouble."

Then we're alone.

Damian opens the rear door of his vehicle and shoves me inside. My limbs are like lead weights and won't respond. To keep the nausea at bay, I shut my eyes, but the world continues to spin until it fades away completely.

Chapter 9

Violation

Gunshots fire from somewhere nearby, then shouting. I force my eyelids apart, blinking several times to clear my vision. Where am I? I swallow but can't open my mouth. It's taped shut somehow. I reach to yank it off, but something sharp is binding my hands together, and they're tethered above my head.

Adrenaline kicks in and I scream, but with my lips bound, the sound is pitiful even to my own ears. Thrashing and kicking doesn't result in anything more than pain tearing into my wrists. I struggle against them, but the bindings only dig in deeper. It's hard to breathe, and my lungs constrict, making each breath a little harder to take in through my nose. *I'm going to suffocate.*

Pins and needles cover my skin, and the room spins in a dizzying whirl. I close my eyes and lift a silent prayer. *Help me.*

A calm settles over me, and I relax, pushing down the instinct to fight.

The shouting morphs into a song. I recognize it as a commercial for the soda I drank at dinner. *The drink.* I went to the ladies' room. The PE teacher warned us in health education classes about date rape drugs being snuck into unsuspecting women's beverages. I never thought it would happen to me. Damian seemed so nice. And I'm a fool.

A television sits a few feet away, hung above a grimy, dinged-up dresser. The sound is up too loud for normal. It's a bedroom, and I'm lying on a king-sized bed with a rough cover over me and a musty pillow under my head. The blanket is too scratchy, and I suddenly understand why. My clothing is gone, and my naked skin crawls with the sensation of the surrounding filth.

I remember nothing after Damian closed the SUV door, but my body tells me he's taken something from me I'll never get back. Though my brain is a blank slate, my aching carcass informs me about what happened while my mind slept. A tear slides down my face and soaks the pillow. I don't know exactly what he did, but I don't need to know. I don't *want* to know.

Mom will be so disappointed in me. Jenny will have every right to say, "I told you so," and they'll both be correct. I'm as dirty as the surrounding room, inside and out. If only I could scrub my poor choices and the resulting night away in a hot shower.

I use my knees to draw the covers tighter and inhale a whiff of Damian's cologne. It sends a shiver down my spine.

From now on, I'll never forget the reek of evil.

No time for self-recrimination. I need to break free before he returns.

Once more, I struggle to sit up, and the rope connecting my bindings to the bedpost tightens. Instead of fighting it, I employ it to pull myself up. The disgusting blanket slips away, the air cool against my exposed skin.

I stand beside the bed. Now what? The cable loosened somewhat in my effort, and I have enough length to move in a compact circle.

With my new status of being upright, the room tilts. How long have I been out? Where is Damian? If I shout, will he turn up? Or would a maid hear and rescue me?

Blackout curtains cover the wall by the door. If I manage to reach them, perhaps I could open them and signal someone walking by. The room is so dim I can't tell if it's night or day.

I force my brain to slow. To calm. *Think, Nova. What can you do?*

Using the bedpost as a scraping tool, I try to remove the adhesive strip covering my lips, but the broad band and smooth texture tell me he's used duct tape of some sort, and he's wrapped it around my mouth and head a few times. Frustrated, I let out another muffled scream and ignore the angry tear that trails down my cheek.

Find another way, Nova.

If Damian brought my phone into the room, I could use it to call Mom. To dial 911. With it nearby, Mom should be able to track me down. We have an app that shows where we each are. Yes. It's a matter of time. *If* he left it here. Would I be that lucky?

It isn't a large room, and I scan every surface in view. The only thing the grungy furniture holds is dust.

An open door on the far side reveals a toilet and a sink. Most likely, a tub is around the corner. Thoughts of showers remind me of how dry my mouth is. Water would be a gift right now. But each path to it lay cut off. What if Damian never comes back? Will I die here, in this room? How long would it take for dehydration to suck the life out of me?

No. You can't think like that.

I'll break free. I have to.

The scratch of an old-fashioned key being inserted into the lock draws my attention, and my breath catches, my heart slamming against my ribcage.

He's back.

Chapter 10

Chaperone

The door opens, and sunlight streams in, blinding me until it's closed again. My eyes readjust and focus on a woman who stands between me and my freedom. Her coal-black hair is pulled into a snug ponytail, and her dark jeans and T-shirt belong in some sort of spy movie. Her olive skin could make her Damian's sister. Toned arms say she works out, and she towers at least six inches taller than me.

Without a word, her eyes sweep over me from head to toe, slow and measuring, like a seamstress sizing up a bride she already knows won't fit the dress. A chill prickles across my arms, and I fight the urge to shrink under her gaze.

She pulls a switchblade from her back pocket and snaps it open with a flick. The metallic click echoes off the walls, somehow louder than a gunshot above the noise of the television. So, this is it. My final day on earth.

Police will discover a youthful, broken body. Female. Late teens. One of them will wonder where love went wrong for someone so young to meet the end. Will they be able to identify me? Will Mom get the chance to lay me to rest? To grieve?

No. I won't give up.

I tear my attention from the blade and scan the room, desperate for something, anything I can use to fight back. Nothing. Just me—barefoot, bruised, and furious.

If only he'd left my shoes on. I'd shatter her teeth with one solid kick.

Bare feet will have to do. She's about to learn that volleyball players don't only have heart. We have legs that can take another person down.

Something in my posture must give me away. Her eyes narrow.

"I'm going to cut you loose," she says, her voice a warning. "Don't make me do something we'll both regret."

Hope flickers. Can I trust her? If she's here to help, why hasn't she shouted for backup? Why hasn't she called the police? If she's lying, I've got one shot. One chance to attack, with my hands still tied, against someone armed and ready.

The odds are terrible. But so is waiting to die.

I brace myself, heart pounding.

Please, God. Let this be my opportunity.

And if it isn't…

I'll fight anyway.

She closes the distance between us, and adrenaline spikes through me, tightening every muscle. The blade catches the weak ceiling light, flashing cold and sharp. She reaches toward me with it, and my lungs seize.

Should I strike first?

Her arm sweeps down and slashes the cord tethering me to the bed. My arms fall free.

The sudden release throws off my balance, and I sink into a heap on the floor.

Before I can react, she grabs a handful of my hair and jerks me up. The blade's flat edge grazes my spine, icy against my bare skin.

"I'd hate to be wasteful," she hisses, "and Damian would be furious. But if you try anything, I'll bury you."

I freeze, every muscle locked in place, silently begging her to put the knife away. A tear slips out, tracing down my face. Whether from terror or the savage tug at my scalp, I can't tell. It doesn't matter. A groan rumbles from me.

She gives my hair another brutal jerk, her mouth so near that her breath mists against my ear, damp and inescapable.

"You gonna behave?"

The pressure on my tresses eases enough for me to nod.

At last, she lets go.

Relief surges through me, quick and dizzying. I'm not free—not even close—but I'm still breathing. For now. I swallow hard and cling to the thought: *Patience. Lord, help me find a way out.*

Hands on hips, she levels a glare at me. Heat flushes my face and neck at her assessment, like I'm a frog pinned under glass in a high school lab.

I twist, desperate to cover my nakedness, but with my fists bound I can only shield one part of myself, leaving the rest exposed to her cold observation. Bile climbs in my throat as my breath catches in a strangled sob. I want to curl in, to disappear, to melt into the floor until I'm nothing but a shadow.

But I didn't choose this. I never gave her—or Damian—this right.

"I'm your chaperone," she says, her voice flat. "That means I'm either your new best friend—or your worst nightmare. Your choice."

Chaperone. The word scrapes against my mind, almost laughable in this situation. Damian, the swine, left nothing to protect.

She snaps the blade shut and tucks it back into her pocket with a flick of her wrist. Arms folded across her chest, her nose wrinkles like she's avoiding the air I breathe. She sniffs, lips twisting. "You stink. Like him."

The name—*him*—curls off her tongue like it leaves a foul taste behind.

Without warning, she shoves me toward the bathroom, leaving me off balance so I stumble. "Time for a shower."

This will be my chance. She'll take off the plastic cuffs and the tape sealing my mouth, so I can wash. That will be my moment. I shuffle to the doorway and cringe at what I find inside. A yellow-stained sink with cigarette burns on the laminate, a cracked wooden toilet seat, and a shower with missing tiles. Plus, enough mold to win a prize in the school science fair.

Chaperone steps into the doorway—arms crossed. "I don't have all day. You've got fifteen minutes to get cleaned up and do your business."

I hold my hands out toward her, willing her to understand. *Take the cuffs off.*

She shakes her head. "Fifteen minutes." Without turning the water on, she turns and strides off. The sound of channels switching tells me she's planted herself in front of the television to wait.

Above the filthy sink, a large mirror, cracked in one corner, reflects the truth. Bruises mottle my skin, each one explaining the relentless ache pulsing through every inch of me. The girl staring back isn't me. Wild, matted hair sticks out from beneath duct tape, eyes wide and empty like a madwoman lost in the dark.

A tremor runs through me. I tear my gaze away, spinning around, desperate for something that might offer a way out. But the bare walls grant no mercy. No window. No back door. Only these four suffocating facades.

With shoulders sagging, hope slips away. There's no escape. No rescue. I'm alone, and my world is breaking.

Chapter 11

Unbroken

No way I'll give in to despair. I'll escape somehow. But first, I need to get *him* off me. Chaperone is right about one thing. I stink.

My wrists scream in protest with each twist of the shower knob, and I dream of doling out some of the same discomfort to Damian or Chaperone.

No.

More.

I want to scratch and gouge. The lesson from the youth group's Sunday message comes back to haunt me with the thought. Turn the other cheek. Right. *You'll have to prove that one to me, Lord.*

I relieve myself while hovering over the filthy toilet seat, flush, then pivot to test the temperature. Little more than tepid, though I'd turned it to the hottest setting. Better than cold.

Though the yellow-stained curtain looks like it's hung there since the sixties, I drag it aside, enter, and close it behind me for a few precious minutes of privacy. The instant the water hits my skin, a shuddering wave of relief courses through me. It's as if the filth of Damian's touch peels away with each drop.

A tiny, half-empty shampoo bottle sits next to a sliver of soap. I flip the cap open and squeeze some onto my head. But my hair is so tangled in the tape, and my hands so clumsy inside the plastic cuffs, I can't manage more than an awkward scrub. Each attempt leaves strands snarled and yanked. If I keep going, I'll end up with a bald patch from tearing my own hair out.

Surrounded by water, a sudden thirst slams into me. My tongue's swollen, coated in paste. When did I last drink anything? Probably that soda Damian bought me. The one he must've drugged. Fresh anger surges, a flash of heat in my soul. It holds back the rising tide of panic.

Like a greedy desert in need of a rainfall, I'm desperate for life-giving fluids. The water could loosen the adhesive. I shove my face under the stream, working at the edges with my nails, scraping and picking. The tape clings as if he's cemented it in place. Tiny flecks come off, but nothing more. My breath hitches. Desperation claws at my sanity, and I dig faster.

I need a drink. I need air. What if Chaperone comes in and stops me? How long have I been in here? Why didn't I think of this sooner?

My fingers tremble, grating harder while I yank at the thick film bonded to my cheeks. Who cares if I scratch myself bloody? My heart pounds so hard it hurts.

Suddenly, I can't pull in enough oxygen. My lungs constrict, each breath more shallow and useless. My head spins, the room tilting and shrinking around me. *Oh God. No.* Not now. Not here.

The shower tiles blur. My legs weaken beneath me, knees wobbling. I sway, clutching at the slick wall for balance. A greenish haze presses inward, closing in, suffocating. I can't pass out. I can't. But my body isn't listening.

Not . . . now . . .

Chapter 12

Caged

A thousand pinpricks race over my skin like ants crawling across my arms and legs. My head throbs, and a high-pitched ringing fills my ears.

The shower curtain whips open. A blast of cold air hits my wet skin, shocking me upright. The world sharpens into focus. Chaperone looms over me, her icy stare pinning me in place.

Words fly from her mouth. Curses, shrill and rapid-fire. I fight to steady my breathing, every uneven heartbeat jarring through me. She twists off the shower and yanks a phone from her back pocket.

"You here yet?" she barks into it.

A man's voice crackles through. "Pulling in now."

"I need the box."

My vision clears further, and I realize she's staring directly at me, her cheeks flushed, jaw tight. Anger radiates off her in waves.

I suck in a shaky breath. I'm still here. Still alive. But for how long?

She jerks me up by the biceps. "Stand."

The force of her tug drags me to my feet, but my legs buckle. I crash to my knees, chin smacking the sticky tile with a jolt that sends stars bursting behind my eyes.

"What a klutz," she sneers. "Can't even walk right."

A thud sounds somewhere in the central room. My eyes flutter open enough to see her boots retreat. Her voice floats back to me. "I said I need the box. Are you deaf?"

A man's tone rumbles back. "Chill. I'm getting it."

Footsteps shuffle closer. She's back, a blanket draped over one arm. She crouches beside me, hooking her free elbow under mine. "Up."

With her help, I wobble to a standing position, legs shaking above the wet, urine-scented floor.

She wraps the barrier around me, tucking the edges into my bound fists. A rush of unexpected gratitude hits me. She isn't going to parade me naked in front of some random.

But almost immediately, the thought curdles. What am I doing, feeling grateful? She doesn't deserve that.

Once I'm draped in the heavy fabric, she strides away into the larger room. "Come."

What am I? A dog?

The bitter thought flashes through me, but I shove it down. I don't want to risk angering her again. I want to keep the cover.

Like a whipped puppy, I follow.

The moment I step into the room, my heart lurches into a wild, painful rhythm. Propped against a moving dolly stands a large cardboard box, its side flaps folded open instead of the top. Inside, sits a metal cage, its door yawning wide, waiting.

I freeze, every muscle locked. My chest squeezes. Breaths came in shallow, rapid puffs. If I pass out again, they'll take the blanket. I can't lose my shield.

Squeezing my eyes shut, I force myself to inhale at a slower pace, counting each breath, willing my pulse to steady.

Not now. Stay upright. Stay calm.

A sharp crack, flesh slapping flesh, snaps me back to the present.

Chaperone stands rigid, glaring at a big, heavyset man in a leather jacket. His black skullcap tugged low. Thick, tattooed arms covered in wiry hair. His scruffy beard can't hide the sour scowl twisting his lips. A patch on his coat reads one word: Outlaw.

She jabs a finger toward me. "You know the rules. She's off-limits. So wipe that thought from your tiny brain before I smack it out of you."

He shoots her a defiant glare. "Lookin' doesn't hurt nothin'."

"Looking leads to temptation," she snaps, turns her icy gaze on me. "Into the cage. *Now.*"

My feet retreat of their own accord.

Chaperone sighs a venomous sound. "Didn't think so." She steps aside, jerking her chin from him to me. "You know the drill."

The enormous man's heavy boots thud across the floor. He moves past her, closing the distance between us.

Tears blur my vision. My entire body trembles, shaking so hard my teeth clack together.

Not the box. *Please, God, not the box.*

Suddenly, I'm in his arms. He hauls me to the bed, unfazed by my thrashing, and flops me down, face-first. His hairy body pins me, his weight pressing me into the mattress.

"Stop fighting," he growls near my ear. "You're gonna hurt yerself."

But I don't give up. I twist, buck, and squirm with every ounce of strength I have left.

There's a pinch in my arm. The sudden sting of a needle shoved deep. My breath hitches. What did they give me?

The fight drains from my limbs. Something slow and heavy, like syrup, spreads through my veins. Big Guy scoops me up again, and his arms tighten around me. He stuffs me into the cage and slams the latch closed with a metallic snap.

"Sleepy time," he mutters. His voice fades, and the world grows muted.

Panic slips from my body like sand through a sieve, replaced by an eerie, unnatural tranquility. I know, deep down, the last thing I should feel is calm. But I can't hold onto the fear anymore.

The flaps of the box shut and seal me in darkness. My eyes sag, lids too heavy to fight. Helpless, I let obscurity take me.

Chapter 13

Lily

There's an argument nearby. A couple fighting. Did Dad show up again? It's been ages since the last time he barged in, reeking of whiskey and demanding time with me. But . . . the female voice doesn't sound like Mom.

My eyelids won't cooperate. They hang heavy, like stubborn curtains refusing to rise for the start of the show.

I roll over, hand fumbling for Super Fluff, but my purple pillow isn't there. Must've fallen on the floor overnight. Time to get up anyway. I can't afford another tardy. One more and it's detention.

With effort, my eyelids surrender and crack open. The room swims in a blur. I sit up and rub my eyes, shivering when the blanket slips away and cold air brushes against me. Wait. Why am I naked?

Panic stabs through me. I never sleep without PJs. Never could.

And it hits me. This isn't my room. The weight of reality crashes over me, squeezes the oxygen from my lungs. Damian. Chaperone. Big Guy.

Where am I?

The argument goes silent, replaced by the chirpy jingle of a toothpaste commercial I half-recognize. A TV hums nearby, but not in this room. I glance around, heart hammering. This isn't the same hotel. Somehow, it's shabbier.

A tiny moan pulls my attention to the bed beside mine. Black braids spill out from under rumpled covers, the strands frizzy at the edges, coiled like soft ropes across the gray tinged pillow. A small ebony hand shifts. In the dim light, green-polished fingernails gleam with each sudden twitch. Red, raw rings encircle her thin wrist. Angry marks that speak of tight restraints. Even in sleep, there's a faint crease between her drawn brows. Her lips part with a muted whimper. I can imagine the nightmare she's having if her reason for being in this room is anything like my own.

My hands are free. I can open my mouth again.

Has someone rescued me? No. If that were the case, I wouldn't be in some grungy hotel room.

My heart pounds as I stumble out of the bed and clutch the blanket around me. A heap of clothes sits piled on a battered dresser. With shaking fingers, I struggle to pull them on, each motion clumsy under pressure.

No shoes.

I scan the room. Nothing. Fine. I don't need sneakers to escape. I tiptoe to the door and reach for the handle . . . something tightens in my chest. *Guilt*. It scratches at my brain, refusing to let go. I can't leave her here.

My heart twists. A wave of nausea rises the moment I look back at her puny frame. She can't be older than twelve. I'd bet younger. Her thin fingers tremble and curl against the covers. The raw, angry marks circling her wrist scream of a captor who hadn't cared if they cut off her circulation.

Dizziness rolls through me. What have they done to her?

I want to reach out. To say something. *You're not alone. I'm here.* But my arms weigh too much, my fear too loud. The knowledge of what Damian did to me, might have done to her, makes my terror snap tighter. More urgent. Not just for me now. For her. I bite down on my lip, forcing back the tears stinging my eyes. No matter what happens next, no matter what they do, I can't leave her behind. But she's too big to carry, at least not easily. Should I wake her?

I twist the doorknob. It turns, but the door won't budge, as if the lock's been disengaged from the inside.

No. *No.*

I jerk the other way, tug, yank, rattle it harder. Still nothing.

"We're not allowed near the door."

The small voice freezes me in place. I turn.

She's awake, pupils huge with terror. She inches herself upright, legs dangling over the side of the bed. Her black T-shirt, loose over her thin shoulders, glints. A silver anime character smirks across the front. Sparkling threads run through her leggings, catching tiny flecks of light. She's so heartbreakingly young. She needs to know she can trust me.

I hurry back and perch across from her so we're face to face. "I'm Nova," I whisper. "It's not safe here. We need to find a police officer who can help us." I reach for her hand, but she flinches and shrinks back.

"Chaperone said she'd put the ties back on if I don't behave," she murmurs, voice trembling. "They hurt."

Her wide eyes fill with tears. One slides down to drip off her chin.

"It's okay." The words taste false on my tongue. Can I really protect her? Not if she won't trust me. "What's your name?" I try again, my tone hushed so as not to scare the frightened rabbit.

Her gaze flicks to the door beside the dresser. There's an adjoining room. "Lily."

"Such a lovely name." I stand and tiptoe toward the door. I press my ear to it. Faint voices, a television.

"How long have you been here?" I ask over my shoulder.

She curls tighter on the bed and hugs a pillow to her like it's a shield against the world. "Two meals."

Not very helpful. Breakfast and lunch? One day? I don't want to push too hard, to scare her off. The floor-length dark curtain beside the door draws me like a magnet. I draw it aside enough to peek out. We're in an old-fashioned L-shaped motel that stretches around a cracked, unpatched parking lot. What must be the office, big front windows dim with grime, sits yards away. Only one vehicle sits parked outside: a plain white van. No logo, no markings. Just . . . blank. Beyond the asphalt, a narrow road cuts past, though I can't tell if it's a single lane or two, but definitely not a highway. On the other side, a pine forest extends as far as I can see. If we escape this room, we'll lose them in the trees. Find help.

The knob on the adjoining door rattles.

Lily gasps. "Quick! Close the curtain!"

I spin, heart lurching, and let the drape drop behind me. The door swings open.

Chaperone strides in, a brown paper bag in one hand, a cardboard drink holder with two cups in the other. Her eyes flick from the empty bed I'd left to me standing near the entrance.

"Away from the window. Now."

Chapter 14

No Escape

Chaperone tosses the bag onto the mattress with a thud, sets the drinks on the dresser, and snaps her fingers. "Bed." Her glare pierces through me like a laser.

My legs refuse to move. Why does she want me there?

She crosses her arms, her mouth a grim line, and calls over her shoulder, "A little help."

Heavy footsteps echo from the other room. Big Guy strides in. His grin, slow and cruel, sends a chill scraping down my spine. "Whatcha need, boss?"

"She won't sit." Chaperone steps aside, eyes cold. "Second lesson in obedience. Go easy."

On the bed, Lily curls into a ball and shrinks against the headboard.

I can't budge. My brain sputters and jams, leaving me frozen in place. Big Guy closes the gap between us. His thick arms surround me, and he hoists me up like I weigh nothing. He tosses me onto the mattress, my teeth clacking together with the impact. In a flash, he zip-ties one hand to the bedpost.

Eyes raking across my body, he looms over me. My body shakes uncontrolled, breath shallow and jagged.

Chaperone? I search for her, desperate. Aren't chaperones supposed to protect? "I'm sorry." My voice cracks.

She nods, lips tight. "Enough. You've made your point."

Big Guy winks at me and backs off.

Relief crashes over me so violently it prickles down my arms, leaving me lightheaded.

With a nod, Chaperone flicks her fingers at Big Guy. "You can leave."

He lumbers out, his jeans swishing with every step. I stay frozen, my heart still hammers but a little slower with each thud fading away. I used to think of myself as tough, strong. All those volleyball practices, gym drills, the times I pushed my body to its limit. But next to her, all taut muscle and coiled power, and him, who could pass as a nightclub bouncer or worse, I'm nothing. I can't fight my way out of this. I'll have to out-think them.

Chaperone points to Lily and then toward the food. "After you finish eating, you can give her the other burger and drink. But not before."

Her eyes slide back to me, flat and cold. "There's no one around to hear you make a fuss, and I can't stand the noise. So keep quiet. If you'd behaved, you'd have toilet privileges. But now you'll have to wait for permission."

She turns on her heel and strides out of the room, pulling the door shut behind her with a heavy thud.

I exhale, the sound shaky and thin. So, this is how it is. Every move controlled. I press my forehead to the bedpost. The plastic bite of the zip-tie digs into my wrist. If I'm going to survive this, I need to clear my head. Control my emotions.

Once they're gone, Lily uncoils from her huddled position, her face streaked with drying waterworks. "I told you," she murmurs. Her gaze darts to the door and lingers, as if waiting for some invisible signal that they'll return.

Several tense beats pass with her fixed in place. She slides off her bed and creeps toward the food bag like she's crossing a minefield. First, she pulls out a sandwich and then selects a drink. With them clutched in her small hands, she scurries back to her mattress as if the floor itself might bite her.

Perched cross-legged, she wedges the paper cup between her knees, peels back the hamburger wrapper with trembling fingers, and sinks her teeth in.

The scent hits me like a punch—rich, greasy, mouthwatering. My stomach growls so loudly I half expect her to react. How long has it been since I've eaten? That fancy burger and fries at the restaurant are only a memory from another lifetime.

I swallow against the cotton clogging my mouth, but it's no use. There's no saliva left. "Can I . . . can I have a sip?"

Lily flicks me a wary side glance, then turns her back, shoulders hunched over her food.

I've never seen anyone eat so fast. Still, every chomp and gulp stretches out like slow-motion torture. It's not until she's licked the last smear of ketchup from her fingers and drained the cup dry with a noisy slurp that she moves again.

Without a word, she tiptoes back to the bag, retrieves the second burger and soda, and places them on the table beside me. It's as if Chaperone burned obedience into her mind.

With my free hand, I seize the drink first, straw between my lips, and pull in the orange soda so fast it's like tasting sunlight after a storm. It's the best thing ever. My stomach growls again, louder this time. I fumble the cup down and grab the sandwich, devouring it in four messy, desperate bites. The soda's gone just as quickly, too few long, greedy pulls.

For a moment, I sit back, my gut aching but grateful. Salt, beef, and sugar still cling to my tongue. But the hunger for safety, for freedom— that's only begun to roar.

Chapter 15

Damian

Time twists in strange ways when you're trapped with nothing to do but wait. My back throbs from lack of movement. The fingers on my tethered hand are cold and stiff, the blood sluggish from being held above my heart too long. I try to flex them, but they're like rusty hinges.

I have no idea how many hours bled away since I woke in this room. The blackout curtains seal the area in a heavy, suffocating twilight, erasing any sense of morning or night.

The television in the opposite room murmurs in the background, a lifeline of sorts. I cling to the sound, straining to make out the words. Not because I care what's playing, but because it's the only thread connecting me to the outside world. Anything to fill the oppressive silence.

Lily retreats into the bathroom, and the trickle of water pouring into a cup fills the room. Her soft slurps reach my ears, each one sharp as a pinprick in my mind. My cotton-coated tongue aches. Swallowing is an effort. I ask her if she'll refill mine too, but she doesn't respond.

Hard to blame her. The poor thing is terrified. A little mouse scurrying through this cage. I'm sure my earlier defiance only made things worse between us.

I close my eyes to fight off the gnawing thirst. If I want to survive, I'll need to win her trust.

She darts back out of the washroom, leaving her cup behind. My shoulders sag. I don't think I could bear watching her sip it like everything was normal. Back on her bed, she draws her knees to her chest, eyes fixed on some invisible point. Waiting. But for what? Neither of us knows. Part of me thinks I'd rather remain ignorant.

Still, I must attempt to build a bridge to my only potential ally. "I'm sorry I didn't listen to you earlier," I say. "You were right."

She flicks a glance at me but doesn't respond. I press on, leaning closer. "Where do you live? When we get out . . ."

Her lips press into a thin line, shoulders curled inward, and her eyes bore into the wall like she can will herself away. She's a fortress.

"I'm going to do my best to keep you safe," I whisper. "You can trust me."

The knob on the adjoining room rattles. Lily sucks in a breath, arms wrapped tighter around her trembling knees. She's retreated deeper into herself, and I'm left sitting here, watching the shield she's built grow taller by the second.

Damian steps into the room, and a hot surge of anger paints my vision red. He's wearing the same stupid jacket I once thought looked good on him. The one that now reeks of betrayal. His spicy scent hits me like a gut punch. I want to claw the smug grin off his face.

He saunters closer, ignoring Lily's soft whimpers. "Already causing trouble, huh?" His voice mocks me. "Didn't take you for the rebellious type."

I shoot him a glare sharp enough to slice, but he doesn't flinch. I can only dream of a look that would burn him to ash. Instead, he invades my personal space and cups my chin in his palm, his grip firm, hands pressing a little too harsh. "Such a pretty flower. Makes me wonder if I should keep you to myself."

A flash of heat fills my lungs, and the urge to bite his wrist surges through me. His fingers dig into my jaw like a vice, locking me in place.

"You'll pay for what you did to me," I hiss, twisting counter to the restraint.

His grin sharpens, and he grabs a fistful of my hair, forcing my face up to his with a rough jerk. "Oh, you think you're some kind of victim?" His breath is hot on my cheek. "You wanted everything you got. Don't pretend you didn't."

I wrench against the tie holding me, heart pounding, but his words strike harder than his fists ever could.

"You really think your mother would welcome you back now? After what you did? After how you acted?" His lip curls in a sneer. "You're no better than a streetwalker. Just as used. Just as filthy."

My stomach lurches, bile rising in my throat. How can I face Mom again? My friends? What will I tell a future boyfriend or husband someday?

He's right. It's ruined.

I'm ruined.

"Hands off." Chaperone's voice cuts through the room like her blade. She stands in the doorway, eyes cold, one hand slipping behind her. I hope she's going for a weapon.

Relief surges through me the moment Damian lets go of my face and steps back, palms lifted in mock surrender. "Simply talking. No harm done."

She waves him off, unimpressed. "Move."

With one swift, practiced motion, she pulls the switchblade from her back pocket, snapping it open with a metallic click.

Chaperone advances on me, and my instincts scream to recoil, but I lock myself still, refusing to give them the satisfaction.

The blade flashes once, slicing through the plastic binding me to the bedrail. My arm drops like a dead weight. The blood surges back into my fingers, sending dozens of needle pricks through them. I grit my teeth, clench my hand into a fist, then shake it out, forcing the feeling back into the limb.

She leans in close, eyes narrowed. "Bathroom privileges—for now. Step out of line again, and you're back in the box."

Without another word, she turns back to the other room, shoving Damian ahead of her. "Don't wear out the merchandise. You've already knocked the price down with your little night of fun. The bruises still haven't faded."

Damian glances back at me, and the raw hunger in his eyes shoots an ice-cold shiver straight down my spine.

Now I get it. I understand why she's here. And worse, I realize exactly what they're planning.

My pulse thunders in my ears. They scream at me to run, to hide. But I'm trapped. Helpless.

My gaze falls on Lily, curled in her glittering pants and cartoonish shirt, quivering on the other bed. My throat shrinks, and my heart cracks open. How will we ever escape?

Chapter 16

Sisters

When I walk into the bathroom, the stench slams into me. Sour, bitter. My stomach lurches. The chipped porcelain and stained sink don't help. I press my lips together, inch inside, and catch sight of the unflushed toilet. I gag and jerk back a step.

Fantastic. No plumbing.

On the slim chance Lily simply forgot, I jab the handle. It creaks and rattles, but the sludge doesn't budge. With a finicky commode at home and a single mom struggling to support us, I've grown proficient in minor repairs, including persnickety toilets. A glance into the lidless tank tells me why: not a drop of water.

My socks stick to the floor in spots, and I grimace at the yellowed tiles streaked with grime. The damp air weighs thick, as if the walls have soaked up years of filth and ooze it back into the atmosphere.

Still, standing here gagging won't fix anything.

I step back into the hallway, gulp a few deep breaths, and steel myself. Back inside, I crouch by the bowl, twisting the valve underneath. It sticks, then jerks loose, but no hiss, no flow. Desert dry, either way.

Fine. If the water's off, I'll do it the old-school way.

It takes a half-dozen trips between the sink and the tank with my drink cup in hand, the old faucet sputtering and groaning with each refill. I finally press the handle, and the toilet gurgles, then flushes with a loud, triumphant roar.

Relief prickles through me, sharp and unexpected. One minor victory. At least we won't have to sit in our own filth.

Now that I can breathe without gagging, I scan the room with fresh eyes, not for comfort, but for possibilities.

The hazy mirror sits fused to the wall, as immovable as stone no matter how I tug or pry. Useless. No blow dryer, no iron, not even a plunger. Nothing like the hotel bathrooms from volleyball tournaments. The curtain rod stands bolted in place, solid and unforgiving.

Then, I see it. A small window above the tub, no wider than my shoulders. Sunlight seeps through the grime, turning the glass vomit yellow. Still, it's the only hint of the outside I've seen since peeking out the front.

I climb onto the tub's ledge and grip the soap dish and the curtain rod for balance. The porcelain is slick, but I steady myself and lift up, muscles straining. My arms tremble with effort, but the training from volleyball, all those pull-ups and bar work, kicks in. I manage to hoist my head high enough to peek through the haze.

Trees. Endless trees stretching out behind the motel.

No buildings. No cars. No people. Just the forest swallowing everything in sight.

They chose this place on purpose.

I drop back into the tub, my breath shallow. The window doesn't open. No latch. No hinges. Even if I could hold myself up with one arm long enough to strike it with the other, there's no guarantee I could break through or fit through the opening if I did.

But Lily might.

A flicker of hope stirs, faint, but stubborn. She's so skittish, though. My little mouse, unwilling to meet my eyes. Would she try?

I'll have to convince her.

Because if that window's our only way out, it's going to take both of us. I can't do it alone.

Back in the larger room, I find Lily curled into a ball again, knees tucked into her chest, arms wrapped like a shield.

"I fixed the toilet." I keep my tone soothing and gentle and sink onto the edge of my bed. "We'll just have to fill the tank each time we use it, but hey—it works."

Her wary eyes track me.

There must be a way to gain her trust. "Do you have any brothers or sisters?"

She gives the tiniest shake of her head, but it's a thread of connection.

"Me neither," I say, tucking my legs under me. "It's only me and Mom. Always wanted a little sister, though."

Her arms loosen a fraction. Her eyes, still cautious, hold a flicker of curiosity. Progress.

"Would it be okay," I venture, "if I treated you like a sister? We could look out for each other. You know—protect each other."

A gunshot cracks from the television in the other room.

Lily flinches. Her body jerks like a spring recoiling.

Slow and steady, I push off my bed and lower myself onto the edge of hers, near but not crowding. I rest a light hand on her arm. "It's just the TV," I murmur. "You're safe for now."

To my surprise, she doesn't resist. She gives the smallest nod.

"Wish we could watch," she whispers, voice thin as paper.

One sentence. The most she's said yet. My fists clench. "I love cooking shows," I say, with a smile. "Especially those crazy baking competitions with the enormous cakes. What's your favorite?"

"Cartoons," she says on a breath, so soft I have to lean in. "Anime."

"Oh, I'm into those too."

Careful not to startle her, I shift my hand to her shoulder, rubbing small, gentle circles. The way Mom comforted me as a child.

"I'm going to do my best to take care of you, Lily," I breathe. "We'll figure a way out of this. Together. Okay?"

Her eyes glisten, the shine of unshed tears making them too large for her face. One slips free. She swipes at it fast with her fist. "Okay."

Chapter 17

Dog

I ignore Lily's warnings and her wide, fearful eyes and ease against the adjoining door, pressing my ear tight to the wood. Damian's voice cuts through, smooth but sharp-edged. Chaperone's shriller tones snap back. If they'd turn the TV down, I might catch more.

Damian's accent rises above the blaring commercial jingle. "We can't deliver two when we promised three. He said no contact until we have them all. One transaction."

My heart tightens. Lily and I aren't their only targets. Somewhere out there, another girl is about to be pulled into this nightmare. *Please, God, keep her safe.* Every moment they're stalled is one more for me to figure a way out.

Chaperone's voice bites in return. "That one's getting too hot to hold onto. They're running press conferences, candlelight vigils. Couldn't you have picked someone less . . . visible?"

Is she talking about me? Or Lily? Mom must be frantic by now. If it's me, maybe even Dad's been told. If he has, the fight between my parents might never end.

Damian scoffs. "He wanted clean-cut. You know how tough that is to find these days?"

A loud argument erupts on the TV, muffling whatever she says next. I pull back, heart pounding. This is the most I've learned all day, and I've nearly been caught twice already.

It may be time to stop. I need to focus, not on their words, but on finding a way out of here.

Perhaps I'll return to the restroom. Stare at the useless window and pray a miracle escape plan drops from the mildew-stained ceiling tiles.

Shouts from the other side of the door make me pause.

Chaperone's shrill tone cuts through first: "Don't let it in. Oh, come on."

Then Big Guy answers, his voice low. "What? It's friendly. Reminds me of the mutt I played with as a kid."

"It's probably crawling with fleas."

The doorknob moves. I leap away, tossing myself onto my bed like I've been there the whole time. Lily stiffens beside me.

The door swings open, and Big Guy lumbers in, the usual greasy brown paper bag in one hand and a drink tray balanced in the other.

Behind him, a small tan terrier squeezes through the door and bounds straight for Lily as if it's returning to its favorite spot. Its ears perked, tongue lolled in a lopsided grin, it leaps up onto the mattress, licking Lily's hand, then her face. She strokes its head, and the dog melts under her touch, wriggling closer with full-body joy.

Each time Lily pets it, the tail wags faster. Her lips twitch, then curve. A genuine smile. Not the cautious, clipped kind. Something open and filled with wonder.

The bag lands in my lap with a greasy thunk. Big Guy's gaze latches onto the pup, a soft grin tugging at his mouth.

"Yup," he says, almost to himself. "Just like my old boy. Always happy to see people."

Lily glances from the animal to him, her voice a whisper. "Can I keep it?"

Chaperone barks from the other room. "What's taking so long in there?"

Big Guy frowns and leans in enough to murmur, "For a little while." With a swipe down the dog's furry back, he turns to leave.

I blink in disbelief. If there is a heart in that massive chest, I'd bet it beats more for the mutt than for either of us.

Still, I'll take it.

The door clicks shut behind him, and Lily exhales.

"I've never owned a dog." She runs a hand over its fur, and it flops onto its side, tail wagging like windshield wipers in a storm.

"Me either." Another odd thing we have in common—no pets, no freedom, and trapped in a nightmare.

But watching her light up, I sense we won't be strangers for long.

We eat the cold burgers in companionable silence. The dog's arrival lightens the atmosphere. A small moment of joy in a world of anguish.

Gratitude wells in me for this scruffy little ball of fur. It's like a God-wink, a quiet message from above. *I see you.*

I reach across the divide, holding out the last bite of my burger toward the pup. "Here you go, buddy. Final bit's yours."

He snaps it up so fast, I half expect him to choke. I stroke his head, and my hand brushes against something slick. A leather collar. My pulse skips. He has an owner. A wild thought sparks. What if . . .

I glance around. Dresser, nightstand, both empty. No pen, no Bible, no paper. The bag will have to do. I flip it over, and a ketchup packet falls out. Perfect.

Not wanting Lily to see, I slip into the bathroom, easing the door closed behind me. Giggles float in from the other room, somehow settling my nerves. I tear off part of the bag's flap. It's thin, but better than nothing. With careful precision, I puncture a corner of the ketchup packet and squeeze, testing the red liquid on toilet tissue. The first attempt blurs, but the second reads somewhat legible. The third time, I used the bag as my canvas and manage a shaky HELP US — IN MOTEL.

I layer toilet paper above. Though the goop spreads a bit, the words are readable. I take a quick peek around the doorframe at Lily. She's preoccupied with the pup. Next, I roll the note into a strip and tuck it in my pocket.

Back in the room, Lily's face is lit with a rare smile. The animal wiggles in her lap and gives off a shrill yip.

"Shh," I murmur and stroke its head. "We don't want to upset Chaperone."

Lily flinches, shoulders tightening, glancing at the door.

"Can we name him?" She whispers.

"Hm . . ." I scoop the dog up, heart thudding. "What's a good name for a fellow with such a busy tongue?"

Lily giggles. "Kisses."

"Kisses, huh?" The hound wriggles in my arms, tail thumping.

The doorknob wiggles. Lily's head snaps toward the sound.

"Don't forget to get that mutt out of there," Chaperone calls, her voice muffled by the door. "I don't want fleas in my bed."

As Lily's attention locks on the door, I slip the note from my pocket and slide it under the collar, catching the loop with trembling fingers.

Please, God. Let it hold. Let it reach someone.

Chapter 18

Emergency

Lily's soft snores rise and fall, each breath loosening the knot in my chest since she finally surrendered to sleep. Poor kid. Exhaustion won. The television still blares from the other room. Some late-night show with canned laughter that doesn't belong here. My mind races in the quiet. Kisses, the note, the chance to escape. And yet . . . no footsteps, no voices, no doors slamming shut for hours. Only the flicker of the television's glow under Chaperone's door. Could they have left?

I inch toward the window, heart thudding against my ribs. If they're here, they're probably asleep too. I hesitate at the curtain. The fabric is heavy, stiff, reluctant to move. I slip two fingers through the seam and part it a fraction. No light leaks through the grime-caked glass.

I draw in a breath and slide behind the drape, letting it shroud my shoulders like a cloak. I peer outside, my forehead touching the cold pane.

The pale moon hides within a veil of clouds. For a moment, darkness thickens, swallowing the world beyond the window. Then the orb slips free, casting a faint glow across the crumbling hotel lot. Shapes emerge—the edge of the building we're in, a sagging bench, cracked pavement, and weeds curling from the sidewalk. I turn my face, cheek pressed to the chill of the glass, scanning left and then right along the row of doors.

Empty. No cars, no forms moving in the shadows. Not even a cigarette tip glowing in the dark.

My breath fogs the window. Maybe . . . we're alone. Possibly we're crouched here in the gloom, terrified of chains that have already slipped loose.

I let the curtain free from my fingers, its weight drawing it into place with a faint whoosh. I cross the room. At Chaperone's door, I press my ear to the wood. A late-night preacher's sermon drifts through the thin wall, the words sharp and deliberate, as if aimed straight at the hollow in my chest.

"Listen, folks, Christ didn't set you free so you could sit in a cage with the door wide open. No—it is for freedom that Christ has set you free!"

A solid thump fills the air. I can almost see the minister's fist slamming against his Bible.

"I don't know who needs to hear this tonight, but don't let your past failures define your future. No one is beyond redemption. You are a precious child to your Heavenly Father, no matter what words your earthly father or mother ever uttered over you. No matter what you've done."

A dry laugh catches in my throat, bitter and uncomfortable. If only he knew.

No. I force the thought aside before it can sink its teeth in. Regret can wait. Right now, I need to focus.

My hand curls around the doorknob, slick with sweat. Slowly, carefully, I turn it, centimeter by centimeter, until the knob reaches the end of its range. My heart hammers against my ribs, a wild, muffled drumbeat.

Here goes nothing.

Holding my breath, I give the handle a gentle tug, and the door swings inward without resistance.

No way could it be this easy. Then I see it—the second barrier. Adjoining rooms always have two. What are the odds the one on the other side is unlocked too?

There's a knob on this side, for which I breathe out a prayer of gratitude. I freeze, waiting. The preacher's voice rises through the wall.

"I'm claiming freedom for the captives . . ."

A narrow beam of light breaks the dark when the panel shifts under my touch. My jaw clenches with each frantic heartbeat, my breath snagging. Dizziness prickles at the edge of my vision, and my hands tingle. *Not now.*

I close my eyes, forcing slow, measured breaths. In for three, out for three. Again, until I manage five on the exhale without gasping. Good enough. I don't have all night.

I open my eyes to find the gap has widened. The glow of the television spills into the room, flickering through the cluttered space. A king-size bed sprawls across most of it, sheets twisted and empty.

A thin slice of light cuts out from under another doorway. Bathroom. My stomach clenches. Is Chaperone in there? Big Guy? Or are we truly alone? If they're gone, I should test the exit. We might be free and not even know it. I could grab Lily and run. Somehow, it's too smooth, too silent. A snare waiting to snap shut.

The room's a mess. Fast-food bags and crumpled cups crowd the trash. An alarm clock ticks on the nightstand. I spot a shadow blotting out part of the glowing numbers. My breath hitches. Square, small. Could it be . . .

A toilet flushes. *Shoot.*

I freeze. Seconds. That's all I've got.

I dart forward and snatch the object, elated to realize I was right. It's a phone. I spin on my heel, slip through the gap, and click the door into place behind me.

My pulse roars in my ears. Waiting is its own kind of agony. Will they notice? How fast?

Then it hits me. I don't have time to wait and find out. I hurry into our washroom, close myself in with a click, and tap the screen awake.

Chapter 19

Phone Folly

Of course, phones have passcodes. I sit on the floor, my back pressed against the sink. Why had I risked such a maneuver when everyone locks their devices? It's not like I know anything about these people to guess at their code. I've chided Jenny multiple times about using her birthdate for her passcode. Too many people have that date.

Mom uses her phone number from her childhood when cell phones weren't a thing. The day she helped me set up my first bank account, I'd gotten the easiest pin in the world to remember 9-5-9-5, and I use it for everything. Even Jenny and Mom know it. We have no secrets. Well, at least not before Damian.

I can't be certain whether this device belongs Chaperone or Big Guy. What did it matter? Knowing won't help me. From their appearances, they could be in their late twenties, maybe early thirties. So perhaps the year of their birth?

This isn't the time to give up. I tap in four digits. *Incorrect PIN.*

Then a second one, a year later. *Incorrect PIN.*

That's when I spot it—*Emergency Call* glowing beneath the fingerprint pad. Why hadn't I thought of that?

I don't need access to the phone to contact the police. I press on the words and hold my breath. A keypad comes up, and I punch in 9-1-1.

A loud crash from the other room makes me flinch.

Lily's screams cut through the air.

"Where is it?" Chaperone barks.

Lily's cries turn into full-blown sobs, and my breath catches.

I can't stop. This is our only chance. *Forgive me Lily.* I hold the device to my ear.

Nothing. The screen flashes, *dialing . . .* Why won't it go through?

The doorknob rattles, and the door jams into my spine.

"Give it back!" Chaperone's growl turns murderous.

Lily's cries sharpen, and my innards knot. I wish I could protect her. I try to call again, thumb shaking.

Please . . .

A slam hits the door, snapping my head back.

"Open now, or the kid pays."

Dampness blurs my vision. I tap the screen again. Black. Nothing.

Lily's moans turn to screeches that bore into my brain. I've hurt Lily and gotten nothing in return.

"Okay! Stop!" I choke out. "Please!"

I scramble up and open the door. Chaperone stands there, fury blazing in her eyes, fist tangled in Lily's braids, pulling her up to her tiptoes.

"I'm sorry," I shout, and thrust the device toward her.

Chaperone releases Lily, who crumples to the floor in a puddle.

Quick as a lightning strike, Chaperone snatches the phone from my hand and lands a rough blow that knocks me sideways. My ears ring, and a metallic tang coats my taste buds.

Her hand is in my hair, dragging me forward.

"Think you're smart?"

A punch to my stomach lands me on the floor beside my bed, and she's gone. Pain fills my world, as if there's no room for anything but the agony in my gut and the buzzing in my ears. Then she's back. Hands yank me off the floor and propel me upward. Plastic bites into my wrist, and I'm zip-tied to the bedpost once more.

With one last muttered curse, she storms out, slamming the door behind her.

The room goes still, except for Lily's soft, broken sobs. I force myself to breathe.

Lily's crying drifts through the dark, each moan cutting deeper than the last. I curl into a ball, wishing I could disappear. Wishing I could be the girl who didn't just make everything worse.

Chapter 20

Night

Once the pounding in my head fades and my ears stop ringing, Lily's sobs pierce straight through me, each one sharp and jagged, like a knife I can't pull out. My fault.

"Lily, I'm sorry," I breathe, voice barely holding.

For a second, she glances my way, tears streaming down her blotchy face. She turns away, dragging a pillow over her head. A pitiful shield. I can't blame her. If I were her, I wouldn't want to hear from me either.

I press my forehead to my knees, wishing I could disappear, wishing I could take back each reckless action that led us here. She didn't ask for this. She didn't choose this. And now she's paying the price for my mistakes.

Her cries slowly fade, softening into uneven breaths, and finally to the quiet rhythm of sleep. Guilt and relief wash over me in a tangled mix. She gets to rest. Not me, though. I deserve to sit here, wide awake, choking on every awful thing I've done.

I squeeze my eyes closed, but the weight in my chest doesn't lift. Tomorrow, I tell myself. Tomorrow, I must do better. I have to.

Uninvited thoughts of home slip in. Popcorn and movie weekends with Mom, curled up on the old couch, quoting our favorite lines as if we were part of the cast. We can't afford the theater, so we have the DVR packed with classics we love. Just last month, we recorded a midnight showing of *Titanic*. Mom promised we'd watch the whole three hours together, once tax season ends, and she finally earns a weekend off.

Will she end up watching it alone? Will she sit there on that sofa, waiting for a daughter who isn't coming home?

Jenny's voice pushes in, her last words reverberating in my memory. Why hadn't I listened? She'd seen right through Damien from the start. I'd been so desperate to believe someone older, someone sophisticated, could love me. Not the rich girls or the influencers on social media—plain old me. No money, no famous name, no magazine-cover looks. Just Nova, who should've known better.

The days blur together in my head. One thing I'm sure of is that I've missed youth group. Our leaders, Caleb and Emma, probably kicked off the night with a round of Would You Rather. Laughter would have echoed through the room. That's always one of my favorites. And the snacks. Emma's legendary death-by-chocolate-chip cookies, the ones everyone races to grab before they vanish.

What if they played Minute to Win It tonight? Jenny and I are unstoppable with marshmallow and pretzel stick towers. No one can beat us.

Once that's over, they'd split into two groups, the girls with Emma, the guys with Caleb. Then the real discussions start, the kind you wouldn't share in a big crowd. Emma makes you feel safe, like you're important, no matter how small your question or worry.

Why hadn't I leaned in more? Why hadn't I asked those questions when I had the chance, or let myself believe they could be my support system? Instead, I'd hovered on the edge, half in, half out, too afraid to trust the very people who would've been there for me. Who could have filled in the gaps when Mom couldn't be there.

Mrs. Wells, Jenny's mom, always tries. I can picture her on game nights, not only cheering for Jenny, but yelling my name too. I'm part of their family. *Was* part of it. That time I twisted my ankle at an away tournament, she'd sat with me for hours at Urgent Care, keeping my mom in the loop, making sure I felt cared for.

The support. The love. All along, people watched out for me. Unfortunately, I'd ignored it. Pushed it aside and sprinted straight into the biggest mistake of my life.

The night of my injury, Mrs. Wells shared her favorite verse with me. I think it came from the Old Testament. Something like, "Fear not, for I am with you." It brought comfort while I sat there with my ankle throbbing. Tonight, it presses into me. Why would God be with me? I don't deserve His help. I've wrecked everything.

Next, Emma's voice drifts through my memory, soft and steady. I can almost see the circle of girls at youth group, fidgeting on the floor. The time Katie Hearn, the pastor's daughter, from one of the most prominent families in the area, finally spoke up. She'd been grounded from anything except church activities for stealing lipstick from the drugstore. Small town, smaller church. Everybody knew.

Emma went around the ring, asking for prayer requests. When she'd gotten to Katie, the girl crossed her arms snug to her middle and mumbled, "I doubt God wants to hear from me this week. Dad hasn't spoken to me in days."

Rather than scold or correct her, Emma simply nodded. I couldn't remember her exact words. Something along the lines of: "There's nothing too deep, too wide, too strong that can keep us from God's love."

I recall the way Katie's eyes filled with tears, the way her shoulders loosened a little. Here in this dark room, my own eyes sting. For the first time in forever, something stirs under the weight pressing me down. Something small, trembling, but alive. Perhaps . . . perhaps God hasn't stopped listening after all.

My parched tongue aches for a sip of water. Thoughts circle in my head, only making it worse. The words slip out in a whisper. "God, if you're there. . . I'm sorry."

There's so much more tangled in my head. The urge to plead for help, to ask why one reckless mistake must cost me everything. No further thoughts come.

A quiet wave rolls through me, and warmth stirs in my soul. Not loud or overwhelming, but a gentle heat. Tender, the way Mom's arms felt when she wrapped me in a hug after a long day. It fills the empty, aching places inside me. I breathe without the weight pressing down.

I know what it is. I know who it is.

He forgives.

The realization cracks something open in me and drops slip down my cheeks. Now comes the harder part. Learning to forgive myself.

Chapter 21

Last Chance

Morning must have arrived. I can't tell from the light or the hour. Instead, voices alert me. An argument, too raw and unpredictable to come from the TV, drifts from Chaperone's room, and snaps me out of the thin, uneasy slumber I'd drifted into. My wrist throbs from the zip tie's bite, the ache pulsing up my arm. I shift, stiff from sleeping upright against the bedpost. My neck screams in protest.

I long to crawl closer, to press my ear to the door and catch every word. Across the room, Lily burrows deeper under the covers, her small body tense even in sleep. I don't dare wake her or offer a plea to help me listen. Not after what I did. Not after the damage I've caused. It'll take more than whispered apologies to rebuild the bridge I've burned.

The shouting grows louder, angry words slicing through the thin walls.

Chaperone: ". . . before it's too late . . ."

Damien: ". . . almost have her . . ."

The timber of his voice jolts through me, a cold tremor rippling down my spine. His arguments strike a chord. *Almost have her*.

A third girl. Another life tangled in the same snare. My breath catches in my throat. *Please, God, help her be stronger. Smarter.* Let her see the trap.

The adjoining door bangs open, and Damian strolls through like he owns the world, Chaperone shadowing him with a smirk. The noise shocks Lily awake, her small frame jerking upright, face filled with panic.

Damian sweeps his gaze over her trembling form, a flicker of amusement in his eyes. Then his attention lands on me. "Not much longer, sweetness. Soon you'll both have a new friend and another home."

Chaperone snorts. "And be out of my hair."

A chill shoots through me.

"Buyer's getting antsy. Need to show him what he's got to look forward to." He pulls out his phone, the smirk on his face making my stomach turn. "Smile, girls."

I clench my jaw, refusing to give him one ounce of the satisfaction he craves. Let him take his pictures. Let him angle that device and tap away like we're merchandise, like we're less than human.

Every snap of the camera is a slap, a fresh reminder of how little he values us. Not as people, not as girls with families and lives and dreams. To him, we're a commodity. My fists curl, nails digging into my palms, the zip-tie biting my wrists. He can strip away a lot, but I won't give him the look he wants. Not now, not ever.

He slides the phone into his back pocket. "Hmmm. You might be too old after all. We'll see what he says. If so, I've got plenty of other options for you."

Chaperone sniffs, tossing me a dismissive look. "You'll need to knock some attitude out of that one."

They retreat to the other room, the door clicking behind them.

Seconds pass. My head buzzes. An electric fury racing through me, drowning out everything else. I push myself up, the plastic stinging against raw skin. Good. Let it bite. I sink my teeth into it, sawing at the tie with every ounce of strength left in me, until the murmur of Lily's sobs pulls me back.

She's crumpled in the corner, her small body shaking with quiet, hopeless tears.

I swallow hard, the anger still burning in my chest. I get it. It would be so easy to slip into the same place, to allow the sorrow to drag me under. But crying won't get us out of here.

I glance at the thick plastic binding me then back at Lily.

No more waiting. No more breaking.

We are getting out of here.

Chapter 22

Shift

Muffled voices float through the wall with bursts of excited chatter, followed by quick dings, then a wave of applause. A man's voice booms, muffled but charged with energy, rising and falling in the exaggerated cadence of a game show host.

Every so often, I catch a burst of laughter, the ovation of an audience, and the fast click of a spinning wheel or the beep of a countdown timer. How can Chaperone watch her vapid entertainment while I sit mere feet away, on the other side of the wall, bound and waiting? The joy of the lucky contestants winning prizes grates on my nerves, so distant from this reality.

I haven't heard Damian's voice in a while, not that I want to. He's probably gone off hunting his next victim. The thought sends a shiver down my spine. Her arrival will mean the beginning of the end for us here. I can feel it.

A sudden pounding rattles the room. Someone's at Chaperone's door. Lily, who's been tugging at a loose thread on her glittery pants, freezes mid-motion, eyes focused on the entryway.

A door creaks open farther away, and Big Guy's low rumble rolls into the room, followed by the unmistakable stench of greasy food. My jaw clenches and lets out a pitiful growl.

"Not that thing again," Chaperone snaps, her voice sharp.

Good. Let her be annoyed.

The scratching at the door propels a jolt of hope straight through me.

And then, like a streak of sunlight breaking through the gloom, Kisses bursts into the room, paws skittering across the worn carpet. He barrels onto the bed and into Lily's waiting arms. She spits out a small laugh, hugging the wiggling, barking bundle like it's Christmas morning.

My heart grows lighter, as if expectation itself padded into the room on four short legs.

Big Guy lumbers in after the eager pup, the usual greasy bag and drink tray balanced in his hands. "Lunch," he grunts.

My nose twists at the scent, but the pain in my wrist serves as a reminder. I won't get so much as a crumb unless he brings it to me.

As I watch, Big Guy's frown softens into a grin, his eyes fixed on the dog slobbering all over Lily. It couldn't be more obvious that he loves animals, even if children have no effect on him.

"Please," I ask, "may I go to the bathroom?"

He flicks his gaze at me for a second, then back to the mutt.

"I think I'm going to be sick," I add. The pitiful whine in my tone rankles me, but I know what I've got to do.

With a loud sigh, he shuffles over. The familiar snick of the knife opening sends a ripple down my spine. He crouches, slices the plastic binding my wrist, and the tie falls away.

A rush of pins and needles floods my hand, but it's still a relief. For the first time in hours, a small crack of freedom empowers me.

"Move it." Big Guy shoves me toward the washroom.

Not wasting a second, I stumble inside. The door clicks shut behind me, and I savor the sliver of privacy. I hurry through the motions, then wash my hands. A loud pounding echoes through the motel. A shiver passes through me. Big Guy's already here. It can't be Damian again, can it? He wouldn't have the third girl yet . . . unless he does. A chill slides through me.

The lavatory door swings open, and Big Guy forces Lily in ahead of him, then steps in and closes the door. His hand clamps onto my arm, then covers my mouth, cutting off my breath. He's such a bear of a man that even a single limb is a vise around me. I can't move.

Lily squeaks, but he yanks her close and silences her with the other meaty palm.

He leans in and growls. His breath is hot against my scalp. "Keep quiet, or else."

Outside, voices drift through the walls, not TV voices, but real ones. People talking. A discussion. My pulse roars in my ears. Is the buyer here? Will they ship us off to some place worse than this?

Big Guy's phone buzzes in his pocket. He releases Lily long enough to grab it. She trembles, frozen.

"You breathe a word and you're dead," he snaps at her, then jabs the answer button. "Yeah?"

Damian's voice crackles through the line, cold and commanding. "Kill the girls."

My heart pounds, choking off what little breath I have. Something's gone wrong. This wasn't the plan. He's supposed to sell us, not . . . not *this*.

Lily's smokey-quartz eyes brim with tears, and she slaps a hand over her mouth, staying silent. I yank at Big Guy's hand, desperate to bite, to scratch, but his grip is solid.

On the other side of the door, Kisses barks and scratches, frantic. If only he were a German Shepherd or a Great Dane, something powerful enough to tear this man away from us. But he's a little terrier with more heart than muscle.

No one's coming.

We have to save ourselves.

I slam my elbow into Big Guy's ribs. He grunts, but instead of letting go, his grasp tightens. His hand shifts higher, clamping down over my nose and mouth, and his other arm lifts me off the ground without effort.

Panic slams into me like a rogue wave. I claw at his hand, nails scrabbling, arms weakening with every second I can't breathe. My lungs scream.

Lily's eyes lock with mine, wild and terrified. I want to beg for her help, plead for her to kick or scream, but I can't even nod.

My legs thrash. I aim for his groin, his knees, but each kick is weaker than the last.

I tried.

At least I tried.

An inhuman screech fills the air, and Lily hurls herself at Big Guy, all elbows and teeth, like a ferocious animal set loose. She must have connected somehow, just enough, because he jerks back with a grunt, and his grip falters.

Oxygen rushes into my lungs, and I gasp, coughing, every breath a gift.

The door slams inward, crashing against the wall. A uniformed officer storms through, weapon raised, his voice like thunder. "Drop her. Now."

His face is tight with fury, glare locked on Big Guy, and for the first time since this nightmare began, I believe.

This nightmare will end.

Chapter 23

Safety

Big Guy lets go. I fall to the floor, my knee smacking the tile. My lungs seize, then drag in air like I've been underwater too long. Lily grabs my arm and yanks, her face reddened with effort, pulling me away from his feet as fast as she can.

"Hands up!" the officer barks.

Big Guy obeys, slowly raising his arms. Lily and I shuffle backward, pressing into the farthest corner of the room. Kisses darts in and around us, barking and nipping at Big Guy's heels like a tiny warrior.

"Turn around and get on your knees."

I drag Lily to me, wrapping my arms about her, the need to protect her surging through me. Big Guy glances over his shoulder. His mouth thins into a hard line, and for a second, I think he might fight. But instead he kicks a huge, booted foot at the dog, then drops to the floor.

Relief crashes through me, and my eyes sting. He missed. The dog's okay. We're okay.

"Kisses, come," Lily whispers, her voice shaking. The little dog scampers straight into her arms and licks her face like he's checking on her too.

We stay huddled together, clutching each other and the mutt, while the officer cuffs Big Guy and forces him to the ground, face-first. Only after the manacles zip into place does the official finally speak to us.

"Come on out, ladies."

I never thought walking out of a bathroom could feel like freedom. But stepping into the open space hits like a jolt of something akin to hope flooding through my veins.

The doors stand wide apart, and Chaperone lies face down in the other room, her arms cuffed behind her back. A female officer hovers over her, one hand on her radio, speaking into her shoulder mic with calm authority.

The officer's eyes meet mine. She nods, then gestures us forward.

The room buzzes with motion. Police filter in, sirens wail outside, and more voices yell out instructions. It's chaos, but it's a good kind. The kind that means rescue. Safety.

A red-haired official, her bun neat, gently takes my arm and guides me toward the open door of a police car. She helps me sit on the back seat, legs dangling out, body trembling from the aftershock.

Another uniformed woman with blonde hair reaches for Lily's hand. "Come with me, honey." Her country accent sooths my jangled nerves.

Lily hesitates, glances my way, then follows, Kisses trailing behind her like a little guardian.

My chest tightens. Watching her walk away makes my heart squeeze. After everything we've been through, after what we just survived, does she have someone waiting for her? Worrying about her?

I turn to the red-haired official. "Can't we stay together?" My voice cracks.

Her expression relaxes, and the lines around her eyes crinkle. "It'll be okay," she says. "We need to ask you both a few questions first."

I nod, but the ache doesn't ease. Something tells me the worst of it might not be over yet.

The ambulance arrives with lights flashing and horn blazing, though everything about me quiets, like I'm alone in a bubble somehow. I sit in the back while an EMT shines a light in my eyes, checks my pulse, and asks gentle, persistent queries. I insist that I'm fine and beg to go home.

But they don't let me go. Don't offer me a phone. But how can I tell Mom what I've done? What Damian did?

Tell her my innocence is long gone?

At the hospital, the female doctor examines me with the same kind, professional concern. I'm so grateful they've sent a woman. I can't imagine a man's hands on me. A woman officer stands nearby, arms crossed but expression sympathetic. My stomach twists. I don't want her pity.

Though I answer the questions I can, I nod when I don't have words. Then comes the one I've been dreading. The physician asks it slowly, carefully.

I know it's time I acknowledged the truth. But my resolve shatters, and I break down.

The tears come, my body shaking. I croak out the story I'd give anything not to tell. I admit what Damian did. Saying it aloud strips me bare, peeling away the last bit of armor protecting me. Like waking up naked with an audience.

There's a flurry of footsteps in the hallway. The officer steps out, and the doctor places a warm hand on my arm.

"We've got a specialized nurse who works with young women like you," she says with a tiny squeeze. "She'll explain the next stages."

The truth makes my head hurt. *Next stages.* I don't want any more stages. I want to go home. To be a daughter again. To reverse the clock and have a do-over.

The door bursts open.

"Nova!"

"Mom." I fly off the exam table and into her arms, the tears returning in full force. We clutch each other like the world might fall apart if we let go.

And for the first time since this nightmare began, I'm safe in the protection of someone who loves me.

Chapter 24

Homecoming

Though it's been months since the rescue, school looks like a foreign country. Mom pulls up to the student drop-off, and the building looms, familiar and unfamiliar all at once. She puts the car in park, stopping the flow of traffic, and I know she's hesitating for me.

Concern crinkles the corners of her eyes. "You don't have to do this. We can take your senior classes at home, with tutoring, the same way you finished your junior year. Start fresh in college when you're ready."

Students stream through the front doors like nothing ever happened. Normal kids with backpacks and earbuds and weekend plans. A horn blares behind us. Someone's impatient to get through the line.

I swallow back bile. "No. I won't let him take this from me too."

Tears well in her eyes, but she nods. "You're right. You can do anything."

Sure. Anything. I exit the car and head toward the school.

Anything except try out for volleyball again.

Anything except spend the night at Jenny's without panicking at two a.m.

Anything except hang out at our favorite pizza place and not scan every corner, every doorway, wondering if he's there.

Though they caught Damian in another seedy motel—before the next girl he drugged could even wake up—I still flinch when I see a dark SUV. The thought sends a shiver down my spine.

Chaperone turned on him and Big Guy in exchange for leniency. She'll still serve time, but not nearly as much as they will. Part of me hopes they'll take a plea deal. The thought of seeing them in court makes my knees go weak.

But I'm here. I'm walking back into the building. Back into my life.

That counts for something.

The freshmen who surge through the front doors look barely old enough to drive a go-kart. Some walk wide-eyed, clinging to their backpacks like lifelines. Others strut in like they've already conquered the school.

I should be one of the confident ones. I'm a senior now. I'm supposed to own this place.

The flash of a jeweled pants' pocket catches my eye, and I freeze. Long black braids bounce behind the girl laughing with her friends. Not Lily.

The ache in my chest returns, dull and familiar. I never got to see her, not like the officer promised.

They said her mom's boyfriend sold her to Damian for a cheap handgun. Just handed her over like she was nothing.

She ended up in foster care while the authorities unraveled the mess. Then they sent her out of state to live with an aunt. I wrote once, saying everything in a letter that I couldn't voice. Her aunt replied, kind but firm: *It's best not to stir things up again. Let it go.*

But Lily's not a sleeping dog. She's the girl who saved my life. And some days, the silence feels like a second loss.

The school security officer stands just inside the doors, his K-9 partner at his side, sniffing students filing past. The dog's presence might have rattled me before, but today it grounds me. I like dogs now.

My phone buzzes in my pocket, and I pull it out. The lock screen lights up: a picture of me and Kisses (real name Toby) nose to cheek, together looking slightly scruffy and proud. That brave little mutt carried my message through an entire forest of pines and led the police straight to me, with a little help from Mr. McIntyre, Toby's owner. I owe them both more than I can ever repay.

"Nova!"

Jenny's voice breaks through the noise of the morning rush. She weaves through the crowd and pauses a few feet away, like she's still not sure how close she's allowed to get. Then she pulls me into a hug, gentle but real.

"You made it."

"I did." Two tiny words. But they feel enormous, like standing on a podium after surviving the hardest race of my life.

"You ready for senior year?" she asks.

I glance toward the crowded hallway. My jaw tightens, but I nod. "Not really. But I'm here."

She tucks her arm into mine. "Girl, I was born ready."

Thought it wobbles, I give her my best smile.

I don't trust the world the way I used to. I don't move through it with my eyes shut anymore. But I move. One step. Then another. Always forward.

Starting over doesn't mean pretending nothing happened. It means choosing to keep going, anyway.

And I'm choosing to begin again.

The End

Acknowledgments

I dedicate this story to the brave men and women who devote their lives to confronting the world of sex crimes with the goal of rescuing those held captive. My introduction to this reality came through my husband, who served in sex crimes for five years. During that time, he and his team worked tirelessly to dismantle the operations of those who profited from destroying lives for their own twisted gratification. The work demanded long days, midnight phone calls, and exposure to some of the worst evils humans inflict on one another.

This fictional tale draws inspiration from two actual cases that remain unforgettable to me—one from my husband's jurisdiction and another nearby. Though I never personally met the victims, I will never forget them. One young girl did not survive the abuse inflicted by the man to whom her mother sold her. My heart grieves for her too-short life, and I hold fast to the hope that someday all her pain will be healed.

I am deeply grateful to Brave Authors and Sarah Hanks for the opportunity to tell this story, and to my co-authors, B.D. Lawrence and Shannon McNear. I continue to be amazed at how our diverse perspectives and approaches can merge into a unified, beautiful whole.

Finally, my thanks to God and to my family for their constant support—especially my husband, Tom, who endured endless questions as I pestered him for details. Any mistakes in portraying law enforcement fall on me alone, despite his valiant efforts to keep me accurate.

Other Books

OTHER BOOKS FROM BRAVE AUTHOR BOOKS
Every Life Treasured
Every Voice Heard

OTHER BOOKS BY B.D. LAWRENCE
The One-Armed Detective Series
Chilled to the Bone

OTHER BOOKS BY SHANNON MCNEAR
Daughters of the Lost Colony series
Fronteirs of Liberty

OTHER BOOKS BY ANGELA D. SHELTON
Collapse Series
Rise of the Y